SUN IN THE OVEN

PARANORMAL DATING AGENCY

GALAXA WARRIORS

NEW YORK TIMES and USA TODAY

BESTSELLING AUTHOR

MILLY TAIDEN

Sun in the Oven

Published By

Latin Goddess Press, Inc.

Winter Springs, FL 32708

http://millytaiden.com

Cover by: Willsin Rowe

Edited by: Tina Winograd

Formatting by: Glowing Moon Designs

SUN IN THE OVEN

Henley Rourke is a woman who loves a challenge. A while back, Gerri Wilder convinced her and two friends to make an interstellar jump to another galaxy. A thrill too hard to resist, Henley found herself on a planet filled with gorgeous shifters. But she's restless and looking for a little adventure. And then she meets Damen Iceri. Badass. Shifter. Oh, yeah, and so hot, he makes her undies disappear. She gets more than she expects when she realizes Damen isn't the only hot shifter who wants her.

Gunner Lukas, alpha of the Summit Bear Clan is a pair with Damen. Gunner is also the alpha to Damen's omega. Bound by tradition and ritual, these two bears are looking for their mate, the one woman to complete their triad. And that's Henley. But he's not sure how she will handle finding out. When this triad gets together, things go from hot to explosive.

They're ready to make their mating dreams come true along with all the dirty thoughts she's had since meeting them. A forever threesome? All about her? Yes, please! But there's no time to think about forever—not when they are charged with finding the source behind a series of deaths by poison and doing their best to keep Henley from becoming the next victim.

— For the adventure-seeker in all of us. May you find your own happily ever Alpha.

ONE

"Is the old bastard awake yet?" Vander Kasaval didn't turn around. He kept his gaze from his rooftop oasis on the bustling market and the sand ocean beyond. "Last report said he was stirring, opening his eyes." He turned to his Chief of Security. "How am I expected to serve my people as their king if I can't get to the bottom of this conspiracy? It's been almost a year, Damen."

Damen Iceri moved to the king's side. The pressure they were dealing with would cripple most men. "You're serving the Palladian capital and the people of Galaxa just fine, Vander. This situation isn't a 'one and done.' It's got tentacles and roots that spread like I've never before seen. We've made progress.

"If anything, the people have seen you act decisively. You, Jag, and me included. Maddox was one of your own. No one thought the Lord Chamberlain of the Palladia would turn traitor and kill the ones swore to protect and govern in your name. As hard as it was to do, you handled it by showing no one is above the law. As for the tentacles, we're finding them and dealing with them one by one. Maddox is a major key."

"A major key." The king exhaled. "If we can get him to talk."

Damen squeezed Vander's shoulder. "Not if, but when. He's in and out of consciousness, so I haven't been able to question him too much, but he was lucid enough the last time to realize his fate."

Vander snorted. "What? That I plan to rip his balls off and feed them to him once we wring every last piece of information from him?" The king exhaled, raking a hand through his long hair.

"I know it's hard, V. Maddox served the royal house of Kasaval for generations." Frustration bit into his gut at the strain on the king's face. Vander was counting on him, and he wouldn't let him down. "Maddox served your father as Lord Chamberlain before you. His treason is hard to understand. Especially for you and Jag. Your brother is ready to do more than rip the man's balls off. He's ready to go medieval on his ass."

Jag walked in from the inside garden. "You got that right. As long as I get my hands around his skinny neck, you can wring whatever else you want from him," he replied with a frown.

"Yeah, but I'm king, so I get first dibs." Vander glanced over his shoulder at his brother, a smirk on his face.

Damen gave the king's shoulder another squeeze. "Let us handle Maddox. You've got enough going on right here at the castle. Ivy is ready to give birth any day now. You've got enough to worry about with her wanting to have your heir back on Earth. Thank the suns Jag got together with Riley. She and Gerri Wilder are the only ones who can talk your mate down these days."

"Tell me about it." Jag nodded with a wink. "Riley has a heart as big as Galaxa. She's a godsend in more ways than one, and as for Mrs. Wilder, our resident matchmaker has put her other clients on hold until the baby comes."

Vander's eyes met his brother's gaze. "To think I didn't want to use her Paranormal Dating Agency services. We'd all be fucked right now, and not in a good way. Gerri has matched so many warriors both here and on Nova Aurora that King Alyx Transvaal and I discussed giving her a permanent place on both our respective councils."

Damen stifled a wince. Mrs. Wilder on the king's Privy Council would not go over well with the career politicians. Vander looked his way, curious. "Something on your mind, Damen?"

"Other than you making my life exponentially harder by putting your matchmaker on your council so I have to deal with the butt hurt egos? Nope," he replied with a wink. "Piece o' cake."

Vander grinned. "What...I thought you liked the silver foxy lady."

"I like Gerri fine." Damen shrugged. "She's one of my favorite people, but I can feel the headache coming from the castle complaint crew. The scheming assholes love their bullshit gripes and their plots to get ahead."

Jag smirked at his brother's head of security. "That's why V pays you the big bucks. Besides, I think Gerri's one of your favs for a totally different reason. From the way you and Henley Rourke have been eye fucking each other lately, it looks like our matchmaker hooked another shifter for one of her girls."

"Fact, dude." Vander nodded.

Damen stiffened. "Yeah, that's not going to happen. Not now, and probably not ever." His tone was definite.

"That was quick and dismissive." Vander

turned to face him. "Don't tell me you think Earth girls aren't worthy, because that would be bad, very bad, considering my queen is from Earth."

"Of, course not!" Damen balked.

Vander eyed him, skeptically. "Good. Otherwise, I'd have to have someone else question my former Lord Chamberlain. Maddox's treason stemmed from his fucked up ideology about keeping Galaxan blood pure. He'd rather we die as a race than mix with humans."

"You mean die at his hand," Jag added with a frown.

Damen's scowl deepened. "I get so angry thinking how many of our women died because of his poison that I physically have to calm down before questioning the man. We've gotten deep into his chain of deceit, but we haven't gotten to the bottom of it. The source."

The king turned for the jug of ale on the iron and glass serving table. He poured a glass, gesturing with the cup. "I should let Henley question him with you, Damen. She's got serious skills when it comes to getting people to talk, at least that's what Ivy says. That one is a fighter looking for a reason to brawl." He paused. "Kind of like you."

Damen ignored the bait. His two best friends didn't understand. Then again, how could they when he never explained. He never had a reason. Until now.

"Henley's a killer combo." The king continued with a smirk. "Or maybe you already found out what that tall, curvy drink of water has to offer, *hmmm*?"

Damen shook his head, trying not to let on how much he wished that were true. "I don't know if I should punch you or laugh," he said, trying to deflect the question. "I think Ivy's crazy has gotten you nuts as well."

Vander gave his friend a small smile. "Dude, you have no idea. If Ivy doesn't calm down, I'm going to have to knock her out until the baby comes, and she knows it too."

"She's just scared, Vander," Jag added. "Riley let slip a little of what they talk about when I'm not around. Ivy has no frame of reference about childbirth Galaxan style. She wasn't there when her cousin Cassie gave birth on Nova. Apparently, on Earth they paralyze mothers before they give birth. Something called a spinal."

Damen's brows pulled together. "You mean on purpose?"

"I know, right?" Vander chuckled, draining his glass. "And some consider us barbaric because shifters exact pleasure and pain when we claim our mates."

"I think you're worrying for nothing. Ivy's tough and sassy like all of Gerri's girls. She'll be fine," Damen replied, glad they were off him and onto the queen and her imminent labor. "Plus, she has you. You'd walk through fire for her the same way Jag would walk through flames for Riley."

"Damn straight." Jag nodded.

Vander moved to pour himself another cup of ale, offering one to Damen, but his security chief shook his head, distracted. "Nah...thanks anyway. I need my wits about me, but you go ahead. You're gonna need it."

"More for me then." Vander lifted his glass to his lips. "So, you gonna tell me what your comment meant?"

Damen tilted his head, knowing he was being purposely evasive. "What comment?"

"*Not now, and probably not ever,*" the king repeated, eyeing him. "It's not like you to be so cagey. At least not with me. What gives?"

Damn. And they were back to him.

"Gunnar," Damen replied before moving to the window with Vander's heavy stare weighing on his back.

"The Summit Clan alpha?" Jag questioned. "I thought you squared things with him a long time ago, Damen? What are you telling us?"

He shrugged, but didn't turn. "I never went back."

"What are you talking about?" Vander frowned slightly. "I distinctly remember Father giving you leave for a transport so you could talk to Gunnar and the Summit elders about why you left the clan and came to the palace. This isn't like you, Damen. You don't shy away from anything. I've never met a more fearless warrior. Why would you choose *not* to negotiate with your clan? You had the backing of the king, not to mention you're my oldest friend. You saved my life. There isn't anything house Kasaval wouldn't do for you."

Damen steeled himself before glancing over his shoulder at his friend. "You never met my clan, Vander. The day I pulled you out of that avalanche, I was more concerned with you not freezing to death than anything else. I didn't care what clan elders would think. I was already in trouble for leaving our territory to hunt alone. It was my fault you got caught in that slide, so I carried you down the mountain. You were unconscious, and though it nearly killed me carrying your big ass to the lower steppes, I knew I had to help."

"V is huge on a regular basis, but when he's dead weight? Fuck, that effort alone should have earned you knighthood," Jag joked.

Damen paused with a short laugh. "I didn't even know who you were then, but you were such a comedian when you came to, I couldn't help myself. Everyone I knew was either colorless or too scared to try anything new. You were so full of life, you made me hate the thought of my boring existence. I took my time getting you up and moving again." He shrugged. "You offered me friendship in a way I never had. The Summit Clan is secretive and isolated. I had never met anyone so free and easy. Of course, I know now it's because you're a royal brat and used to being the center of attention."

"Oh man, he's so got your number, bro," Jag laughed.

"Fuck you, both." Vander smirked, but then got back to the point. "But you went back after you got me to the Palladian palace. What happened when you got there? After all this time, you never said."

Damen's grin faded, and he lifted one shoulder against the unpleasant memory. "Everything was different. I had seen what life was like outside our small, isolated world. I wanted to share what I learned. Open our borders and our minds, but our elders wouldn't hear it. I was the clan's omega, and I had no choice but to adhere to traditions that have existed for centuries. While I was gone, the elders had picked a mate for Gunnar and me. In that moment, everything they expected was suddenly too heavy to bear. I refused her. I wanted us to choose for ourselves. To complete our triad with someone *we* wanted."

"And?" Jag asked.

Damen looked at his friends, not expecting them to understand. "And nothing. I was dismissed outright. The elders wouldn't listen to reason and Gunnar refused to challenge them."

"I can't imagine Gunnar wouldn't have backed you on this, I mean what man wouldn't want to choose his own mate, let alone an alpha?" Jag replied.

"We were young." Damen reached for a glass of ale. "I was barely sixteen when I found Vander on that mountain. I can't blame Gunnar for not going against everything he knew and trusted. He didn't know what I knew. Hadn't seen the way the outside world lived. I asked him to come with me. To meet you both and your family, but he refused. After that, the elders gave me an ultimatum."

Vander exhaled. "So, you left."

"I showed up on your doorstep two weeks later and never looked back." Damen's eyes met the king's gaze, and the look on his friend's face told him Vander saw he wasn't telling them everything. It was time to make them understand.

"Look, I never regretted my decision to leave my clan, but as to Henley," Damen continued, shaking his head. "As much as I want what you both have, I can't get involved. No matter how tempted. Like it or not, for better or worse, I am still the omega of the Summit Bear Clan. At least until I kick the bucket. I can't mate, and neither can Gunnar."

Saying the words out loud rocked him a little, and Damen lifted his cup to his lips. "It's been so long, I'm sure Gunnar hates me. That's why I didn't go back when your father offered. The only way peace could happen is if I returned and took up my role as omega and allowed the elders to decide my life. I'd rather be alone." He clicked the inside of his cheek, shoring up his bravado. "Besides, nameless sex is a not a bad trade off. I get all the pussy I want without any of the headaches."

"Ha! Just wait until you find your true mate, bro. You think sex is hot now?" Jag whistled. "Not even close, dude. Your true mate will rock your world like no one else. Besides, I know you, Damen. I've seen how you are with me and Riley's kids. You keep telling yourself you're better off, but I know better."

Damen drained his glass. "Yeah, well, even if that's true, I'm not going back to that frozen, insulated world. It's too late. I've changed too much." He winked. "And so has my taste in women."

"Anyone with eyes knows what you like." Vander grinned. "Tall and fully fleshed, with sumptuous curves that make a woman statuesque and regal. From the top of her high, dark ponytail to the toes of her signature black knee-length boots. *Hmmm*, sound like anyone we know? Maybe someone whose hazel eyes track your every move and vice versa?"

Damen refused to take the bait. "You two can stop now. Seriously. No."

"Who knows?" Vander shrugged, ignoring his friend. "Maybe Gunnar has changed, too. You'll never know until you talk to him."

Damen snorted. "Not likely, and not worth the effort. And don't think I can't see the wheels turning in your head. You're thinking if you tell Ivy and Riley, they'll get Gerri on the case with me and Henley, and that'll keep Ivy's mind occupied so she doesn't drive you nuts waiting for the baby to come."

Before Vander could answer, the rooftop door flew open as if on cue, and Henley stood there, chest heaving.

"Speak of the devil." Vander grinned.

Damen's eyes found hers and his gaze dipped over her curvy, statuesque frame, the immediate attraction hitting him like electricity in the air.

She coughed at the intensity of his stare, looking to the king instead. "Vander, it's time. The baby's coming."

The king put his glass down and spared a glance for his security chief. "Not worth the effort? You might want to rethink that, bro."

TWO

"Fuck! Get this baby out! I want it OUT!" Ivy yelled between pants. "Where the hell is Vander?"

"He's coming, babe. I told him." Fear gripped Henley's chest at Ivy's next scream. "He's on his way with Jag and Damen." Her eyes flew to the midwife standing beside the bed. "And what are you, a goddamned spectator? Just waiting around to see if the human splits in two? Is she supposed to be in this much pain?"

Ivy panted, gritting her teeth. "A communal birth. Great. Love it. *Arrrgh!* Gerri! I change my mind! I can't do this...*ow...ow...ow*... SHIT! Get me drugs, NOW!"

"You heard the woman! Do something!" Henley stalked to the side of the bed ready to shake the midwife.

Karis shook her head, wiping Ivy's forehead. "Henley, stop threatening the Doula. We don't have those kinds of drugs on Galaxa, Ivy. I told you that. We do everything naturally."

"What kind of fucking backward planet is this? They have mood walls and sex bots, but no Demerol?" Ivy clenched her fists. "FUCK! I want to go home!" she cried as another contraction took her.

"You can't. Neither you nor the baby would survive the trip. You can do this, Ivy. Just focus," Gerri coaxed. "See that vase of flowers on the dresser? Send all your pain there. The last thing you want is to trigger a shift. You need to deliver this baby in human form."

Riley smacked the older woman's shoulder. "Great, Gerri. Why not scare her a little more? Can't you see she's freaked out enough already?"

Henley wrung out another cool cloth and handed it to Karis. "Haven't you people every heard of an epidural! What about giving her a glass of Sidaii wine…or ten. You know how fast it intoxicates us humans."

"We're crowning!" the midwife motioned for the birthing chair. "Help me get her up."

Pushing panic aside, Henley rushed for the specialized chair and placed it at the end of the bed. Vander came through the door as the midwife helped Ivy from the bed to the chair. His handsome face paling at the sight of his mate.

"Ivy," he murmured, rushing forward. He went to take her hand, but she slapped him away.

"This is your fault, you giant shifter sex maniac! You and your freakishly large dick and freakishly large genes....*ahhhhh*!" Her face contorted and she grabbed his hand, squeezing.

Vander's eyes bugged and he hissed. "Holy vice grip! She's breaking my fingers!" He glanced at Damen and Jag, still in the doorway. "Wipe that grin off your face, Iceri, or you I'll order you to hold her other hand!" He winced. "FUCK! OW! Ivy!"

"Break' em all, Ivy. Just for being a smartass," Jag teased, moving to give Riley a quick kiss before getting out of the way.

Karis smirked, wiping Ivy's brow. "What's the matter, my King? You look a little pale."

"If you weren't the closest thing to being my mother, I'd—" Exhaling hard, he sank to his knees. "FUCK!" he ground out again.

Ivy grinned between pants at Vander's expense, and Henley let out a breath. Maybe everything would be okay. "*Aww*, the big, bad lion king can't stand a little finger squish? Try switching places with your wife, buddy."

Ivy screamed and all humor left the room at

the agony in her voice. Sweat poured down her face as she squatted, bearing down.

"That's it, Your Majesty. Push. Push hard!" the midwife nodded.

The Doula squatted as well, one hand on the queen's belly and the other disappearing between her legs. "Listen to me, love. I don't want you to tear, so hold your breath and count to ten in your head. Control your push until I say, then bear down with all your might."

Ivy screamed again, and the midwife reached with a thick cloth just as the baby slid from Ivy's body. Vander's face was unreadable. Worry. Fear. Anticipation. Love. All rolled across his eyes in that one moment.

"It's a boy! A prince!" Karis clapped, but the midwife ignored everyone as she wiped the baby's face, clearing his airway. With a quick smack, a strong cry sounded and she grinned, looking up.

Ivy burst into tears and Vander leaned his head on her shoulder, kissing her sweat sheened skin. The midwife handed the baby to Ivy, skin on skin, for just a moment before handing the baby to Karis.

Henley's arms were around her middle at the raw beauty, her eyes stinging wet. She had never imagined herself as a mom, but this was so real, it was hard to ignore the tug at her heart.

"We're not done, Your Majesty, but I think the king and his friends should leave for this next part." The midwife looked at Vander, her suggestion was not a request and he knew it.

Karis nodded as well and he inhaled, letting go of Ivy's hand. "I'll be right outside with Damen and Jag if you need me," he kissed his mate's cheek and brushed her hair back from her damp forehead. "I love you, Ivy." He spared a glance for Karis as she gently swaddled the baby in a diaper and blanket.

Henley hurried to the door, her eyes finding Damen. She caught him as he watched Karis care for the infant. Was it her imagination or was he just as moved and freaked out by the tender miracle?

He turned at that moment and she coughed, covering herself with a quick chin pop. "Buy the new daddy a drink. He looks like he could use one."

As she closed the door, Ivy cried out again and Vander whirled on his heel only to find it slammed tightly.

The three men stood on the opposite side of the door. "Wow, V. That was some shriek. Think there's another one?" Jag asked, glancing at the barred entry.

"Your guess is as good as mine at this point." Vander raked a hand through his hair. He hesitated as if unsure if he should stay or go, but no sooner did he open his mouth than a guard turned the corner heading straight for where they stood outside the door to the royal apartment.

"What is it? Can't you see we're busy here?" Damen ground out.

"You left orders to inform you the minute Maddox stirred again. He's awake," the guard stuttered.

At the news, Damen whirled on his heel ahead of the others, steeling himself. This was it. This was his element. Justice and retribution. Not babies and mates and things he couldn't have.

The three rushed out with the guard close behind. They clambered down the stone steps to the infirmary, barely stopping for facial recognition as the doors to the locked quadrant opened. Two guards and two nurses looked up from where Maddox lay shackled to the bedrails.

"Your Majesty," the charge nurse acknowledged, inclining her head. "The prisoner is fully awake. The doctor just completed his assessment. He's lucid and in control of his faculties, enough for questioning."

Maddox turned bloodshot eyes to the king as he approached. He didn't flinch, just blinked as if trying to decide what to say.

"Maddox, I'm glad to see you recovering," Vander said, keeping his voice even.

The old man kept his gaze steady. "Pleasantries? I thought you'd hope for my death, considering I traded your wife to Bors."

Vander's jaw tightened, but Damen squeezed the king's shoulder to steady him. He knew Maddox well enough to grasp his ploy. If Vander lost his temper and killed the old man, it was game over as far as intel was concerned.

"Ivy's fine and Bors is dead," the king replied. "You've been in a coma for quite a while, old man. Not only is Bors dead, but so are your accomplices, Tar Navam, the Serene Lord of the Sands, and his henchman, Sharan Dul."

At the mention of the three culprits, Damen's jaw tightened. Together they managed to terrorize the castle and the whole of the Palladia with poison deaths and the specter of kidnapping. And it wasn't over. Not until every last drop of information was squeezed from Maddox. Damen's hands itched to wring it from him personally, but cooler heads prevailed.

"That's right." Jag nodded. "Your partners in crime tried to infiltrate the palace and lost. Desperate men do desperate things, so they changed plans and pulled the same bullshit ploy as you, taking my mate to try and force the king's hand. I tore them to pieces, just as Vander did with Bors."

"Poor Maddox." Vander shook his head, giving the old man a phony pat of support. "Your buddies really threw you under the bus, to use a human phrase. You have no one left. It's just you and me." He slid his gaze to Damen and Jag before looking back to his former Lord Chamberlain. "For the time being, anyway. There are a lot of people who'd like to get their hands on you."

A nurse walked toward them carrying a black glass vial. "The doctor said this would clear away any lingering fuzziness."

Damen whispered to Vander and Jag, "It's an Earth drug called sodium pentothal. Supposed to be some sort of truth serum, or at least that's what Henley told me. She said it's frowned upon on Earth, but that certain government agencies still use it as a tool to gather intelligence from reluctant captives. I asked Mrs. Wilder about it, and next thing, she had it on her following jump from Earth."

Vander nodded. "That one can be a little scary, sometimes."

"Tell me about it." Damen snickered at the thought of the classy older woman. "I gave the serum to the doctor for when Maddox woke. In

21

case his memory needed a bit of a jog. I promised the queen we wouldn't torture him to loosen his tongue…Yet."

The nurse moved to pour the contents from the black vial into a dispensing cup, but before she could, the doctor walked in through the lab door at the back of the ward and motioned for her to stop. "I need to speak with the king."

She nodded once and put the glass bottle on the medical tray at the end of Maddox's bed, and then moved to see to another patient. The doctor signaled for the three men to follow him into the lab.

THREE

"He's beautiful, Ivy," Riley cooed to the bundle in her arms as she handed him to his mother. "He's the perfect blend of you and Vander."

Henley peered at the baby from where she sat on the edge of the bed. "At least he's a normal size. With the way you screamed, I thought for sure you were giving birth to a large toddler!"

"I know, right?" Ivy grinned, looking at his tiny face peeking out from a soft blue blanket. He yawned and she giggled. "I'm so happy, I feel like I'm going to burst."

Hen smirked, skootching over to make room for Riley. "No, babe. You already did that." She shook her head, amazed. "I still can't believe it. Babies are tiny, but damn. *That* came out of *you*!"

"He's not a 'that', Henley. He's a perfect

shifter baby." Gerri chuckled from the other side of the bed. "You still haven't told us what you and Vander decided to name him."

The baby fussed and the midwife moved to the side of the bed and helped Ivy sit up straighter. "You need to nurse him, Your Majesty," she said.

Ivy nodded, allowing the midwife to help her get settled. The baby latched on and she winced as the Doula draped the nursing coverlet over her shoulder. The woman then filled the silver cup on Ivy's night table before holding it out to the new mother.

"Whatever this is, you better keep it coming. I don't feel a thing below the waist," Ivy said, taking the small chalice like goblet.

Henley laughed, finally able to relax. "Better not let Vander hear that or he might take it personally."

"*Ew!*" Riley winced crossing her legs. "Ivy just pushed a watermelon-sized person out her hoo-ha! If I were you, I wouldn't let Vander anywhere near me for a long time!"

Henley's grinned. "You say that now, Ri, but the walls of this palace are pretty thin. Sound carries, hon, and that boy makes you purr. Loudly. I'd give you three weeks before you went looking to raise your tail for pet lion prince. "

"Okay, on that note, let's change the subject back to baby names. Vander told me he wants to name the baby after his father, Jareth." Karis wore a proud grin. "He would have been so pleased."

Henley's eyes were on Ivy's face as she winced, changing the baby to her other breast. "Hurts?"

"Surprisingly, yes." Ivy adjusted the baby, flinching yet again.

The Doula tutted. "It's only until you get used to it, Your Majesty. Some women even find it pleasurable after a while. Drink more of your elderflower juice. It'll help."

"Well, with the way Galaxan men love a nice rack, I'm not surprised." Henley snorted. "Bottoms up, Ivy. You'll be good to go top and tails. You should save some of that magic juice for when you're green lighted to do the horizontal mambo. Think of the fun toys you can try without wincing!"

Karis gathered the stained sheets and towels and handed them to the nearest servant. "Leave it to Henley to make nursing a baby sound X-rated."

"Hey, I'm not the one who said it's pleasurable." Henley chuckled. "That came straight from your baby maven over there. Personally, I'd rather have the full grown version do the honors."

Riley shared a look with Ivy and the two grinned. "Yeah, and we all know who you have in mind for that," Ivy teased. "Full grown with a very full package."

Face hot, Henley looked at her best friends. She could play it off all she wanted, but no one knew her like these two. "Yeah, and?" She shrugged. "Who doesn't like a little eye candy? It's not like I stand a chance."

"Honey, you need more faith in your charms, if you want to work it with that hunka hunka burning bear," Gerri replied. "Damen's hard wired, and if you want to tap that electricity, you need to be the conduit. He's not like Jag or even Vander. Damen has a past that gets in his way."

"What do you mean by past? Like another woman?" The idea of being iced out by a memory made Henley's chest tighten. Damen wanted her. The signals were all there, but if he was unavailable, she'd kick his ass for playing her.

Another servant brought in a platter of fruit and sweets before Gerri could answer. There was a bottle of Sidaii wine and five glasses on the tray as well, and Karis took the platter and placed it on a low table near the empty hearth.

"When a royal baby is born, tradition calls

for a glass of Sidaii to be shared between the women before the men arrive." Karis winked. "Once the men show up, they tend to take over, patting themselves on the back for a job well done." She laughed. "As if!"

Ivy grinned. "Karis, I think we've corrupted you with our Earth slang."

They each took a glass, including Ivy, and Karis raised hers with her eyes shining with unshed tears. "To the joys of motherhood and all the happiness and health you can bear."

Ivy raised her glass, but didn't drink like the others.

"Honey," Gerri began. "It's okay to have a glass of wine. It won't mix with the elderflower juice, and it's not going to affect the baby at all when you nurse. He's got a shifter's metabolism."

Karis smirked. "Unlike some in this room."

Riley poured herself another glass, taking a large donut with chocolate glaze from the tray. "I hope that wasn't directed at me. I'm not the lush of the group." She took a bite of her donut, and chewed, giving Henley a pointed stare.

"Me? I don't think so." Henley lifted her glass still full. "You're on your second glass, Miss Thang. Stella don't need Sidaii or its intoxicating ways to get her groove on, girlfriend. I'm a natural." She snapped her fingers and then flipped her long dark ponytail.

Riley licked chocolate glaze from her bottom lip. "Mmmm...talk about getting your groove on, this donut is almost as good as sex. Ivy, I could kiss you for getting the castle cooks to make them for us. They're amazing!"

"Don't thank me, thank Gerri. She's the one who made the jump with the recipes and ingredients," Ivy replied.

Gerri grinned, watching Ivy hold out her hand for a Boston Cream. "You're both welcome," she said sipping her wine. "So, Hen...you're a natural, huh. How about we put that to the test?"

"Bring it." Henley chuckled as she got up to sit on the couch with her wine. "I'm always up for an adventure," she said turning her attention to the older woman.

Nodding, Gerri tilted her head. "You all know I have my own brand of Spidey senses, but I want to know one thing before I say another word."

"Sure," Henley replied, lifting a hand. She kept her face calm, but her stomach flip-flopped at the way the matchmaker eyed her. Gerri had worked her magic on both Riley and Ivy, but both friends had to go through hell and back first. She wasn't afraid of a challenge, but if Damen's past put him out of the running, who did Gerri have in mind?

"Ivy and Riley are both settled and happy. They found their destinies right here, with a little help from yours truly," Gerri said with a grin.

Henley sat up straighter on the couch, curiosity and unease warring in her chest. "Are you trying to ask me if I've found my destiny on Galaxa or is there something else behind that twinkle in your eye?"

"No, love. I already know your destiny is here on Galaxa. I want to know your heart's desire. If you could create the perfect mate for yourself in your head, and then conjure him right here and now, what would he be?"

"Do you mean what kind of shifter?" Henley asked. "To be honest, I don't really care."

Gerri shook her head. "That's not what I mean. What characteristics would you want in a perfect mate?"

Henley considered for a moment, almost afraid to answer. "I can't say."

"Why?" Riley asked. "You've gone gah-gah over Damen since the first moment you laid eyes on him. The man's tall and gorgeous with a body that doesn't quit, and a job that carries danger more often than not. What more could you want? I'd say he's the perfect match for you." She turned to look at Gerri. "You're the matchmaker. Am I right?"

Gerri swirled her drink. "Perhaps."

"Damen is all that and more, but—" Henley stopped, her face hot as all eyes watched her.

"But what?" Karis asked with the beginnings of a frown on her face. "Are you saying he's not good enough for you?"

Henley put her drink on the table with a sharp glass clink. "I didn't say that. You girls are putting words in my mouth and me into his bed before I've even had a single taste of the man. We worked together when Riley and Jag went off to find Bors and that snake Sharan Dul, and working with him was intense, but—" she stopped again as Karis got up from her spot on the side of the bed.

"Don't look at me like that." She shifted nervously in her seat. "We haven't spent enough time together, and besides, in the short amount of time we had together, I never got that vibe from him." She took a breath at the blatant lie, but it was better to self-protect than be hurt. "Maybe he's just not interested, and if so, why should I give him a second thought?" She glanced from one to the other. "Gerri, you were the one who told me and Riley that Galaxa was a smorgasbord of hotties."

She nodded. "I did, but then again, I have the distinct honor of knowing who should sample that smorgasbord and who just wants to order off the menu." The matchmaker eyed her more closely. "Out of the three of you girls, you, my dear, are the biggest challenge. You like to pretend you're a playah, but you're no ho, Henley. You want Damen, and *only* Damen. Don't deny it. Every shifter in the palace, me included, can smell it on you each time you lock eyes on the boy. He makes your panties wet and your nipples ache, and if you spend any more time eye fucking him, Hen, I'm going to have to make a jump back to Earth just for batteries so your vibrator can keep up. You, dear, are going to give yourself carpal tunnel syndrome with the way you've been taking care of business yourself."

"I have not!" Henley balked, but hid the makeshift brace on her right wrist. "I've been taking notes. Yeah, lots of notes. For when I go back to Earth. I'm going to write a book." She lifted her chin and sniffed.

Riley burst out laughing and shared a grin with Ivy as she gently burped the baby. "A book? Yeah, right. I used to have the room next door from you, remember? Whatever you filled those pages with is out and out porn." She crooked her fingers at the word *pages*.

"Fine. I admit it," Henley said with an

exasperated flop against the back of the couch. "The man gets me hotter than that desert sand out there. I want to wrap my legs around him and ride'em cowgirl. He's just not into me, okay? At least not in the way Vander and Jag were into you two. Happy now?"

Gerri moved to sit beside Henley. She slipped her hand over hers and squeezed. "Sometimes things aren't what they seem, despite the standoffish signals blasting you from all sides. Maybe there's a reason he's keeping his hands and cock to himself."

"Yeah, like another woman." Henley exhaled. "You didn't answer me earlier, so I can only assume you're trying to spare my feelings."

Karis clapped her hands twice. "Okay, Debbie Downer. This is a celebration. I know Damen like I know my two boys, and he's just as cock-driven and mate-determined as Vander and Jag were before they met these two." She jerked her head toward Riley and Ivy. "He's not originally from here, so you might want to talk to Vander. Those two go way back and if there's anyone who can fill you in on Damen Iceri and his wants and needs, it's the king."

Henley shook her head. "I'm not begging any man to want me. Shifter or human. I'm tough and I don't shy away from a fight, but if a man is too dense to want me, then fuck him."

"What if his hands are tied, dear? And not in a fun way." Gerri raised an eyebrow. "Like I said, situations aren't always what they seem, and if you want your situation situated, with batteries not required, then you'd better use that strategic brain of yours and plan your attack. Find out." She shrugged. "What have you got to lose besides that chip on your shoulder?"

"Ooh, Gerri Wilder, matchmaker on a mission. Taking names and kicking ass, calling it like she sees it." Riley laughed.

Henley smirked. "Shut up, Ri."

"So, what do you think?" Ivy asked, rocking the baby in her arms. "You're a smart cookie. Gerri's right. The guys will be back soon. Find an opening and go for the kill."

A slow smile spread on Henley's face. "When you put it that way, how can I resist?"

FOUR

Vander, Damen, and Jag walked with the doctor until he stopped at a bank of microscopes and computer screens. A row of clear jars filled with a brownish slime sat on the steel shelf above the scopes. Damen leaned in for a closer look, jerking back when something inside slithered through the liquid.

"What the hell!" He pulled back with a grossed-out cringe. He'd faced down danger and death, but slithering slimy unknowns made his skin crawl. "If that's some sort of lab pet, you might want to rethink it and get a cat."

The doctor eyed him over the top of his glasses. "It's not a pet. It's what I wanted to talk to you about." He reached for one of the sealed jars and swirled the goo inside stirring the inhabitants into movement.

"These are the worms recovered from one of

Maddox's associates in the market square. We already know he used their excretions to poison the women's bathhouse, causing sickness and in some cases death. In every case that survived, the women were rendered infertile." He put the jar down and then slipped on a pair of surgical gloves before unscrewing the lid. Reaching in with a long set of tweezers, he pulled a specimen from the ooze.

"Oh, man. Do we really need to see that up close?" Jag winced, pulling back as well.

The doctor held the specimen up to a UV light and the damn thing hissed, squirming to get away from the light. Excretions poured from its gray skin into a petri dish underneath.

"Ugh, that's absolutely foul!" Vander raised a hand to his nose. "Must you do that?"

The other two grimaced. "What the hell is that stench?"

"Their excretions." The doctor dropped the worm back into the slime and sealed the jar again. "The foul stench is a defense mechanism. It's the first warning they give a potential predator, but if the predator persists and takes a bite, the next result is a toxin. If you think that stench is bad in here, holding the worms to natural UV light is even worse than the artificial UV lab light. Fortunately, the worms and their excretions only last three days outside their slimy home."

Damen picked up one of the jars and swallowed back on his revulsion, giving the container as swirl as well. "Have you been able to identify the species in our databases?"

Shaking his head, the doctor put the jar on the shelf. "No. It's still a mystery. We did find two pieces of information, though. The first we were able to identify from a sample we took from one of the worms that expired. The source location. These parasites come from somewhere in the central jungles on the far side of Galaxa. We also ran tests on the worm itself, and our analysis was able to read trace elements that left us speechless."

"Go on," Vander prompted when the man hesitated. "We need all the information you can give us."

He nodded, taking a quick breath. "Our analysis found suggestions of shifter tissue in the worm's complex DNA." He lifted a hand, dumfounded. "It's as if the source species had mutated into something completely different." He looked at both men. "The other piece of information we found was completely by accident. One of my lab assistants was careless while working with a live specimen."

"God, please don't tell me one of those gross things squirmed up his nose or something." Jag made a face.

The doctor smirked. "No, but after my assistant's stupidity, I threatened him with that."

"I knew there was a reason I liked you, Doc." Damen winked, relaxing a bit.

"So, what happened?" Vander asked. "Did a specimen bite him? Is he okay?"

The doctor nodded. "He's fine, and no, the specimen didn't bite him. He accidentally pricked his finger with a tweezer while reaching for one of the live worms. His blood dropped into their brown ooze and it was a feeding frenzy. Like a swarm of sharks. They devoured those few drops of blood and then their color changed."

"Their color?" Damen raised an eyebrow, his curiosity piqued. "What, like from green to blue?"

"No. More from a death-pallor to living flesh," the doctor replied. "It was as if feeding on blood charged their life-force."

Vander took the sealed jar from Damen's hand and shook it, watching them slither inside. "Do you think that's the case? That they feed on blood?"

Shrugging, the doctor exhaled. "If you want an educated guess my answer is yes. Do they all?" He shook his head. "That I can't answer. We'd have to do more tests on the few live worms we have left. The ones we have preserved we are going to dissect and infer as much information as we can for the database. Like I said, they don't live more than three days outside that slime. The toxins in their excretions seem to have the same shelf life, which explains why the deaths and sickness at the baths seemed random and confusing."

Damen looked to the lab door and frowned, his fingers curling into his hands, indignant. "Maddox brought these foul creatures into the Palladian capital. Since he never left the city he had to get them from a source." He reached into his pocket for the black vial he palmed from the silver medical tray at the end of Maddox's bed. "Maybe you can't answer our questions, Doc, but with a little help from our friends on Earth, I think we know someone who can."

The three men walked from the lab to the ward room. The doctor took the vial from Damen and poured the contents into the dispensing cup the way the nurse had sought to do earlier. He added a little water from a jug on the tray and then held the cup out to Maddox.

The old man took the cup from the doctor's hand and sniffed. "What is this?"

"Like my nurse said," he encouraged when Maddox tipped the cup to stare at the contents. "It will help."

Maddox snorted. "Help me or them?"

"Just take your meds, old man," Jag chided. "If we wanted you dead, you'd be food for the desert beetles already."

Maddox lifted the cup to his lips and then swallowed the contents in one gulp. He shoved the empty plastic dispenser at the doctor and then slumped onto his pillow.

Eyeing Damen, he frowned. "Whatever that was, it's not going to work. I made sure to make myself immune to whatever mind tricks you might play if I was caught. There's nothing on this planet you can use, so I guess you lose again."

Damen tapped the side of the cup, letting a slow grin spread on his lips. He never allowed gratification to edge into his work, but in this case he couldn't help but gloat. "Maybe nothing on *this* planet." He bent to place the dispenser on the small table beside the bed but leaned toward Maddox's ear. "Then again, who says I didn't import something for this exact situation."

Maddox's eyes locked on Damen as the initial sedative took effect. The old man's pupils dilated and his muscles relaxed into the mattress. Giving a quick nod to the doctor, Damen watched as the man took a syringe from his lab coat pocket and injected the truth serum straight into the bloodstream.

Maddox's lids slipped closed and his lips parted slightly as the drug spread. Damen gave a chin pop to the doctor, and he immediately dismissed the rest of the ward staff.

Pulling the curtain closed, Damen sat on the side of the bed before slipping a lipstick sized cylinder from his pocket. He stood it on the side table beside Maddox's head. "Communicator. Record mode," he commanded.

The cylinder glowed blue, and a white illuminated circle spun at the top of the device. "Record ready."

"Maddox, can you hear me?" Damen asked.

The old man burbled something inaudible, but then nodded.

"Good. I want you to tell us about the worms. The ones from the Tempera jungle, the ones you used to poison the baths."

The old man drooled from the corner of his mouth and the doctor wiped it with a cloth.

"Maddox, can you tell us about the worms." Damen tried again.

The old man nodded. "From the Tempera."

"We already know they're from the jungle. How did he get them?" Vander prompted, but the doctor lifted a finger to his lips.

He pulled the king and his brother to the side, whispering, "Too many voices and too many questions will cause the subject to become incoherent. This drug was formulated for use on humans, not shifters. We have a very short window for it to work."

Vander and Jag stayed back and let Damen handle the questions. The security chief glanced over his shoulder, and the doctor nodded the go ahead to continue.

"Yes, Maddox. They're from the jungle. How did you get them?" Damen asked, keeping his voice steady and calm.

"The nomad. Sharan Dul. He gets them from the Hatun. They give them to him for me."

"The Hatun?" Jag whispered. "They live in the heart of the Tempera. Their tribe is isolated. None of our scouts have ever found their actual settlement."

Damen spared Jag a glance before continuing. "How do the Hatun get the worms?"

Maddox flailed, his head slightly as if in pain. "Hurts to remember."

"Maddox," Damen prompted a little more impatient. "You have to tell me what you know."

The old man exhaled a long breath, letting his mouth drop open with a groan.

"Maddox!"

Damen gripped the man's hospital gown and shook him, but the doctor rushed forward.

"Don't. Violence will only make it harder for you to get him to focus."

"Of course, sorry." Damen removed his hands from the old man, and with a steadying breath, he tried again. "Maddox, how do the Hatun obtain the worms? Do they dig for them near the river?"

A maniacal rasp left the old man's mouth. "No. They trade for them with the Unduru."

Damen exchanged a look with Jag. "Unduru? Are they a rival tribe?"

"Evil." Maddox laughed again, moving his head from side to side. "Unduru feed on the Hatun. The worms are from Unduru bellies after they feed. The Hatun trade blood for the worms so they spare their tribe."

Throat tight, Damen exchanged a horrified look with the others before turning back to Maddox. "Maddox, what do you trade to the Hatun for the worms?"

"Flesh!" he yelled. "I trade them living flesh and blood!"

Damen's fingers closed into his palm and he squeezed, squashing the urge to choke the life from the old man lying on the hospital cot.

"Whose flesh and blood?" he ground out.

Maddox laughed, and the ragged sound

pierced the silence. "Ours!"

FIVE

"Let me kill Maddox now, Vander." Jag clenched his teeth. "It's bad enough Bors and his mountain monkeys abducted our women to sell on the black market, but to think Maddox sold those poor Palladian girls as a hot lunch for those creatures—just to further his sicko pure blood plan?" He raked a hand through his hair. "How have we never heard of this cannibalistic tribe of whatever? I mean, nobody's had Galaxan history drilled into their heads more than us. Why didn't our tutors know about this? Maybe that truth serum stuff made Maddox delusional."

Damen looked out the window at the dark sky. "Maddox may be psychotic, but he's not lying about these creatures." The night was clear, and from this vantage, the peaks of the Mirror Mountains were visible through the cloud cover. "You never heard of them because they've been the stuff of legend and nightmare for a millennium."

"You sound so sure. Is there something you know about this?" Vander asked, interested.

Damen turned from the window. "Yes and no. I didn't know what these creatures were called, but I heard whisperings in the Summit Clan about beings that came in the night and ate shifter flesh." He shrugged. "Gunnar and I always believed they were nothing more than stories told to frighten us and the rest of the clan youth from leaving our land. Remember, the Summit Clan is isolated and secretive and the elders want to keep it that way."

"Yeah, but you're mountain people. Not jungle. How would a hidden Tempera menace affect you?" Jag asked.

Damen fished in a bowl of fruit for a ripe Galaxan peach and held it up. "Because of this."

"Fruit?" Jag asked raising a brow.

Damen nodded. "You said it yourself. We're mountain people. Summit people. Even in the summer when the sands between the capital and the Mirror Mountains are boiling, are weather is cold. We trade for fruit and vegetables we can't otherwise grow ourselves. Each year the elders put together a team to venture down the mountain to the Tempera tribes to trade. Some never return, and the ones that did brought back more than just peaches. They brought back the stuff of nightmares.

"The year before Vander got separated from the royal hunting party and caught in that avalanche, Gunnar and I went off on our own expedition. We decided to find out if the stories from the trade routes were true or not. We left before daylight and made our way down the mountain trails to the jungle. We had no idea where we were going or what we would find, but it was a chance to break free and I took it. I still can't believe Gunnar actually agreed to come with me."

Vander and Jag sat listening. "And?" Vander asked.

"It took days for us to reach the edge of that wilderness. We'd heard the men talk about the trading post enough that we had an idea of where to go. It was deserted. Gunnar and I argued at that point. He wanted to go back, but I wanted to head farther into the bush. He gave in, and to be honest if you asked him, I'd bet he still regrets not pulling rank and making us head home."

"Why?" Jag asked.

Damen put the peach into the fruit bowl and then sat across from his friends. "Because of what we found." His eyes met theirs. "The path through the jungle forests seemed clear at first.

Well-traveled. We passed easily, and there were signs of life everywhere. That first night in the jungle wasn't bad. We found a deserted campsite and bedded down for the night. At first light, we started out again. The path continued as before, but soon enough the trees and roots were less tamped down. Vines twined down from the branches in long, thick ropes, dense with leaves blocking out the sky.

"We walked for hours. The air was heavy and wet and the jungle grew dark, menacing. It was just a feeling—" He shook his head. "There were no warnings. No symbols or signs cautioning us to go back. Just heaviness in my chest setting off warnings that this was very wrong."

Vander nodded. "Your gut. It's what makes you so good at your job."

"I don't know." Damen shook his head again. "Anyway, we needed to find a place to camp for the night, and Gunnar spotted a clearing. Thick trees ringed the spot almost as if on purpose, but by this time we were exhausted and hungry. I ignored the alarms in my head. Looking back now I can see why. That ring of trees was there for a reason."

Jag's eyes found his. "Sacrifice?"

Damen nodded. "Yes. We started a small fire and ate, settling in for the night. I told Gunnar at that point that we'd head back toward the mountains as soon as it was light. His relief was palpable, but what happened later that night haunted me for years. Gunnar fell asleep. In fact, he slept like the dead." He shook his head. "I couldn't shake the feeling that I needed to be awake, alert. That something was coming.

"I remember the fire dying almost as if the air had been sucked from the clearing. I woke Gunnar and made us move to the shelter of the trees. We crouched in the shadows and watched as Hatun tribesmen covered in black and red paint walked into the clearing. Whether they noticed the cooled embers from our fire, I don't know, but they got to their task quickly enough. Three women were tied to the trees across from where we watched. They were stripped naked and then brushed with what I thought at first was red paint like the men. I inhaled, and the copper tang at the back of my throat told me otherwise."

"Blood," Vander replied.

Damen nodded again. "Yes."

"So you saw the creatures, then?" Jag asked.

He shook his head. "No. We were blinded by some force. I heard them, though, and the sounds were awful. Our sight was returned and the clearing was empty of any trace of what happened except for the blood on the leaf bed and the trunks of the trees. Neither Gunnar or I spoke of it after that night. We agreed on one thing, though. Neither of us wanted anyone to come across that place by accident again. We left at first light, and never went back. On our way, we left small marks on different trees just in case we ever needed to return."

Vander inhaled, letting his breath out rapidly. "With as quickly as things grow in that jungle forest, do you think those marking would still be there all these years later?"

"I don't know," Damen replied with a shrug. "All I know is Maddox spoke the truth. Maybe my presence there that night made it worse for the Hatun tribe. Who knows? Maybe they destroyed our markings to protect themselves."

"Protect themselves? Why the hell wouldn't they want to seek out allies to destroy this menace?" Jag asked.

"Again, I don't know," Damen replied. "Your guess is as good as mine. But I also suspect this is the reason we haven't been successful in bringing the warlords to the table with the rest of Galaxa. It's because they're fighting their own battle for survival."

Vander got up to pace. "And now Maddox brought that battle to our doorstep." He turned to Damen. "Do you think you could find that clearing again?"

"Who knows? It's been fifteen years since I left the Summit. I've put that behind me," he answered.

Vander pressed his lips together. "I understand, but now it's time to put this in front of us again. We need to see Gunnar and join with the Summit Clan to eradicate this evil. I'm king. Not just of Palladia, but of all Galaxa. This needs to be done. Not just for the Hatun, but for all of us."

"Vander, I don't think—" Damen began, only to have the king cut him short.

Vander shook his head. "This goes beyond you and Gunnar as alpha and omega of the Summit. You both need to put aside your past and work together." He eyed his Security Chief. "Can I trust you to do this?"

Damen stood with his face tight. "Do you really need to ask?"

"Good. Now all I have to do is break it to my mate." Vander exhaled, raking a hand through his hair.

Jag got up and clapped his brother on the shoulder. "Give up, bro. Your mate just had a baby. You ain't going anywhere. Karis and Gerri will physically tie you down."

"I'm the king. I have to go. I can't ask Damen to do this alone," Vander argued.

Jag shook his head. "He won't. I'll go with him while you hold down the fort here. You need to be in the capital because when word leaks out about these creatures, it'll be you that stops mass panic." He squeezed the king's shoulder. "Just don't kill Maddox before I get back. I want a piece of that old bastard."

Damen nodded with a serious smirk. "Ditto. I want the bastard's heart on a spit."

SIX

"Hey," Henley said, knocking on the half-open door. She waited, keeping a soft smile on her face to hide her butterflies. "Want some company?"

Damen looked up from sorting his field pack. "Suit yourself."

She walked into the large living room. She'd been here plenty of times before, but now things were different. At least as far as she was concerned. So much for being a tough cookie. *If you want him, you're going to have to show him. He's got history...*

After everything Gerri and Karis said, she was still unsure how to do this. Should she pursue him, bold as brass, or hang back letting the signals speak for her?

Damen's apartment was styled along the

same lines as the royal chambers, only smaller, if you could call two thousand square feet, small. His bedroom and private quarters overlooked the far mountains by design, blocking the harsh desert sun.

She leaned on the arm of a high back chair, watching as he packed. "I heard what's going on."

Damen smirked, chuckling to himself. "Ivy?"

"Yup." She gave him a quick smile. "She wasn't happy, to say the least. That is until Vander told her he wasn't going with you."

He glanced over his shoulder. "Let me guess. Riley was next to grumble and that upset Karis."

"Yup and yup." She nodded, trying to keep her mind on the conversation and not his amazing mouth. "Thank God for Gerri. Motherhood has made them both nuts. Ivy's hormonal, and Riley's got it almost as bad though her kids are adopted. Gerri had to remind them this was an exploratory trip."

He zipped his field pack and moved it to one of the stools in front of his bar. "Want a drink? I've got ale and red Sidaii. I think I've got a bag of chips somewhere." He shrugged. "I wasn't expecting company."

"Sidaii sounds great. I need to take a case of

wine back with me. That's if it'll survive the jump," Henley replied.

Damen took a bottle out of the bar fridge and peeled the wax from the top of the cork. He looked at her as he twisted the corkscrew deep, pulling it loose with a pop. "Are you heading back to Earth already?"

"I've been here nearly a year, Damen." She shrugged...well, at least he thought to ask. "Unlike Ivy and Riley, I have no ties to keep me here other than them. If things changed, I might consider staying, but that doesn't seem to be in the cards for me."

Pouring two glasses, Damen's hand froze for a moment and she caught it. He glanced at her from behind the bar before walking to where she leaned on the chair. He was gorgeous. Even a blind woman could see he was a perfect piece of eye candy. From his chiseled face and full lips to his broad shoulders and muscled torso. She took in every inch of his chest, following the line to his hips and the generous package behind his zipper.

He gestured for her to sit on the couch, waiting until she was situated before handing her a glass of wine. He slid beside her. "Cheers," he said, lifting his glass.

Henley touched the edge of her glass to his and then took a sip, letting the sweet wine roll over her tongue.

"So what exactly did Ivy tell you about our trip into the Tempera?" he asked.

Henley swallowed, nearly choking. "Ivy said you were heading to your village in the mountains. Something about clan matters that needed resolving. Vander told her from there you were visiting a trading post on the outskirts, not going fully *into* the jungle. Even I know that's got deathtrap written all over it."

Damen cracked a grin. "The King of Omission." He chuckled shaking his head. "Not that I blame him. If I was about to get a face full from my mate, I might downplay this trip as well."

"Why is Vander downplaying this at all? Are we in danger?" she asked, watching his face. "Then again, maybe he didn't want her to worry. I know I'd be beside myself if it was me." Her voice took on a wistful tone and she coughed to cover herself.

"You and the girls?" he replied. "No. Not at all. But us?" He lifted a hand. "We used the sodium pentothal on Maddox earlier and he told us where and how he obtained the poison for his dirty business. He also told us he traded the women he had abducted to a jungle tribe using them for blood sacrifice."

"*Jesus*…can't Vander send his warriors in to end the practice?" Henley asked, taken aback.

Damen nodded. "Yes, but there's more." He explained what they learned about the worms and what he witnessed as a kid.

"That is absolutely the grossest thing I've heard. Your creatures sound like mutant vampires." Henley's frowned, disgusted.

Damen raised an eyebrow. "Vampires?"

"We have them on Earth." Henley nodded, putting her drink on the coffee table. "Vampires were originally mythology, fictional characters along with shifters, but everybody's out of the paranormal closet now so nothing surprises me, though your gross creatures take the cake."

"Are Earth vampires flesh eating?" he asked.

Henley raised an eyebrow. "No. Zombies, yeah, but not vampires. Vamps drink blood, but they don't have to kill to survive, and they certainly don't require blood sacrifices from the community at large. What you experienced was trippy. It reminds me a little of our ancient Mayans."

"Were they a jungle tribe like the Hatun?" Damen drained his glass and then got up for the bottle.

She shrugged. The conversation had gone all History Channel and she was glad not to think of Damen in danger. "Sort of, but not exactly. The Mayans would hunt and capture their enemies, saving them for human sacrifice to their gods. They weren't offered up as appetizers for some menacing fiend. If anything, the *Mayans* were the menacing fiends, raiding innocents for their own blood lore."

"These Earth vampires, are they invincible?"

Henley lifted her glass for Damen to fill, waiting for him to put the bottle on the table and sit. "Do you mean can they be killed?"

"Yes," he said.

She nodded, acutely aware of Damen's close proximity and how amazing he smelled. "Sunlight is deadly for vampires, and they hate garlic, but mostly you need to behead them after you drive a stake through their heart. To be really sure, though, you burn what's left. Back home, vampires have become mainstreamed so that doesn't happen much. They're accepted.

"Not as much as shifters, but they're getting there. They live off animal blood and synthetic blood supplements. It's cool for the most part, although I do remember there was a coven of vampires a few years ago that tried to establish blood cults. It happened in upstate New York— Blue Creek or someplace. Actually, it was a shifter pack called The Wolfe Clan that brought down the blood club. They are a real sassy bunch."

He smirked. "Like someone else I know."

She caught his intense gaze, and her cheeks flushed. The man was a shifter, so the fact he knew her panties dampened with that look made her blush even more.

"Let me come with you, Damen. I'm stuck in baby central since Ivy delivered. Baby talk and baby things. I need to get out of here for a while or I'm going to go baby-shit crazy! Either that or my own biological clock is going to slap me upside the head and make me do something I'll regret later."

He chuckled. "That bad, huh?"

"You have no idea." Henley lifted a hand. "Don't get me wrong. I love kids. In fact, someday, I hope to have a bunch of my own rug rats driving me to drink, but right now, I want excitement." Damen's eyes stayed on hers and she couldn't look away. "I want the rush. To feel my blood race the way it does when sex is amazing."

He raised an eyebrow, but shook his head. "I know where you're headed with this, Henley, and the answer is no. This is dangerous shit. Way more than even I'm ready to take on. There's no way Vander or I would ever permit you to go, and Ivy would skin us alive."

"Riley and Ivy are moms, now. I know they don't mean it, but I feel like an outsider. Please, Damen. I'm begging you. Let me come." She cringed at how desperate that sounded, not to mention the innuendo he could read into it.

One look at him and she knew the trip to the Tempera jungle was not where his head went when those words left her lips. His eyes dipped to her lips, dropping to the full curve of her breasts and back again. Something changed in his gaze, and when he licked his lips, her mouth watered at how his kiss would taste.

He took her wine glass from her hand and put it on the coffee table, but instead of getting up to show her the door, he sat closer. Slipping his hand into hers, he let his thumb graze her knuckles.

"Your skin is like the softest Palladian silk." His fingers trailed higher over her forearm. "Ironic considering you're such a tough cookie."

Electricity skittered across her bare skin, and she swallowed. Her fingers itched to touch his face, to burrow into his thick hair and beg a kiss. As if reading her mind, he slid his free hand around her waist and pulled her closer. She lifted her face to his, and without pause, his tongue swept her bottom lip, inviting her in for a kiss. She gasped, and in that moment, there was no hesitation.

He brought his mouth to hers and kissed her like a man starved. She moaned, fisting his hair like she wanted. This was what she wanted.

Dreamed of in the dark. Used a case of batteries for… She tightened her grip on the nape of his neck and kissed him deeper, sucking his tongue into her mouth.

Damen pulled back, letting his lips hover close. "You want to come, Henley?" he asked.

"I meant go with you to the jungle, but if you have a different meaning in mind, then I'm listening," she said, trying to play it cool.

His lips spread in a grin against her mouth and he bit her lower lip. "Is that so?" Damen's hand drifted over her belly toward her crotch. "Your scent tells me you're more than listening. You're wet for me already, Henley," he whispered over her lips. "I can smell your sweet slickness and it makes my mouth water for a taste."

Emboldened, her lips spread against his in a smirk. "Just a taste? I figured you for an all or nothing kind of guy." She grazed his bottom lip with her teeth.

A growl formed at the back of his throat. "I want you to come, Henley. Naked. Wet. Begging to come all over my cock."

She dug her hands into his hair even more and pressed her body close. With a growl, he laid her back on the couch, covering her soft body with his hard need. Their kiss deepened, wild and rough. He sucked on her tongue, plundered her mouth, and every moan sent her blood to race.

Damen pushed her knees apart and slid in between her legs, the thin fabric of her leggings letting her feel every hard inch of him teasing her with what lay beneath his zipper. The hard bar of his erection pressed at the juncture between her legs and she moaned, wrapping her legs around his hips.

"Oh, baby, you're so hot," Damen whispered.

She bit his lip again. "I thought polar bears liked it cold."

He growled low in his throat and the rumble was rough and full of desire and Henley's breath caught in her throat.

"Mmmm, the delicious way you smell makes me want to fuck you every time I see you. Do you know how hard it's been not to pull you into the nearest dark corner and have you?"

Damen rolled his hips, letting his hand push her camisole up until the shirt's shelf bra slipped over her breasts exposing her bare flesh. He licked the underside of her jaw to her ear and then trailed his lips past her throat and over her collarbone to the deep valley between her tits.

She arched her back as his lips lingered, her body begging for his mouth. "You're full of surprises, snow bear. I swore we were frozen solid in the friend zone, but here you are hot as hell and making me burn like never before."

"I want to suck you and fuck you every way I can, but my hands are tied, Henley." He drew his chin over one soft mound. "The friend zone is too hard. I can't do it anymore, not with you so close, I can almost taste you, but for me to have you completely…it's…it's complicated."

"Damen—"

He shook his head, but she cut him off. "No. You don't get off that easily."

"With you? I'm lucky I don't come in my pants just looking at you," he teased.

She rolled her eyes. "Ha, ha. You can joke, but I'm serious. You say it's complicated. Okay, then. I think I've done pretty well accepting complicated since the moment I stepped foot on that transport from Earth." She sat up, pushing him back in the process. "So spill."

She shrugged back into her camisole, ignoring the pained look on his face as hard nipples disappeared behind soft cotton.

"I'm not a single entity, Henley," he began.

She scooted back, her hand up immediately. "Wait, are you telling me you're married?"

"No! Wow." He shook his head. "Do you

really think I'm that much of a sleaze ball?"

Looking at him, she cocked her head. "I never thought so, but—"

Shaking his head, he closed the space between them. "There's no but. I'm an omega. That means I'm part of a triad. Me, the alpha of my clan, and a mate we have yet to find. A threesome. So yeah, I'm not a solo gig. It's why I can't have you, not the way I want. No matter how badly I crave every inch of you."

"A threesome." She raised an eyebrow and then reached up to unwind his fingers from the nape of her neck. "Is this something you willingly signed up for or is it a shifter thing? How come Vander and Jag aren't joined at the hip with some other dude?"

At her question, he ran a hand through his hair and shrugged. "Different clans have different traditions. In the Summit Bear Clan, we have and alpha and an omega and together with their mate they form a sacred triad. Neither can claim a woman without the other."

"Claim?" She smirked. "Dude, I've been around the corner a few times, and I know you're not a virgin. You are not saving yourself. So give it up. If you're not into me, just say so. I'm a big girl. I can handle rejection without some blown up excuse."

Damen cupped her cheeks, forcing her to look in his eyes. "This is not an excuse. It's the truth. Gunnar Lukas is my alpha. He still is, and he's as solo as I am because of *me*. I left the Summit. I didn't want any part of our elders picking a mate for us, and I still don't. I haven't been back since I was sixteen years old. That's the unfinished business Vander was speaking of when he told Ivy about this trip."

"Is that all?" she asked. "My gut's tingling, and not because I want to mount you like a horse and ride till morning."

He nodded. "Jag and I are taking a transport to the Summit at first light. Gunnar and I haven't seen or spoken to each other in fifteen years. We need him for this expedition, and he may demand I stay and fulfill my duty to my clan in exchange for his help."

Damen dropped his eyes to Henley's lips for a moment and then shook his head. "If it comes to that, I don't know if I can do what Gunnar wants." His eyes found hers. "Not now, anyway."

His words and the way he looked at her, her heart stopped for a moment. "Why? What's the difference between me and the other women you've had?" She pulled his hands from her face. "Women talk, Damen. They talk a lot. I've heard enough stories about you to fuel my fantasies for the rest of my life. When you made your move tonight, I thought, hell yeah! In the flesh! Now my engines are revved, but the trip's cancelled and I don't understand why."

He slipped his hand over her collarbone, letting his fingers rest above one breast. She inhaled, but didn't pull away.

"The difference between you and those other women is they didn't stir my inner animal. Your presence, your scent, the taste of your kiss has awakened my inner bear. He has slumbered for fifteen years, and now he wants you. Even after all this time and the distance between us, I know in my gut Gunnar feels the stirrings as well, but I refuse to drag you into an unknown."

Damen cupped her breast, flicking her nipple with his thumb. "But there's one thing I can do." He dipped his mouth to hers and kissed her, running his tongue along the seam of her lips. "And that's make your body shake with pleasure."

Letting his hands drift to the tiny straps on her camisole, he slowly pushed them over her shoulders, pulling the soft fabric down exposing her breasts again. This time he dipped his lips to one hard peak, drawing it deeply into his mouth. He let go and moved to the floor in front of the couch, helping her lean back against the cushions.

He slid his free hand over her waist to her hips and glided his fingers below the waistband of her leggings. Henley helped him shimmy the clingy fabric to her ankles, slipping off her flip-flops before kicking her pants to the side. He lifted her camisole over her head and tossed it to the ground as well.

"You're beautiful, Henley," he said, skimming his fingertips over her breasts and down her belly to her shaved mound. "Smooth," he growled, slipping himself between her knees.

She leaned back on the couch as he pushed her thighs apart. His fingers separating the moist folds of her pussy lips before stroking her slick entrance. "Wet and juicy."

"Damen, please…" Her words were a soft gasp.

His free hand moved to the back of her head and he leaned in for another kiss. "Yes," he murmured. "That's it, love. I want you dripping and begging for release."

Two fingers sunk into her slippery cleft and Henley sucked in a breath at the rough feel. His lips clung to hers as he worked her spot, the rough pad of his thumb circling her hard nub.

"Let go, Henley. Tonight is all about you. My hands may be tied for now, but I want to feel you come. I want to lick your slick juice from my palm and fingers. I want to taste you and tease you until your eyes roll back in your head as you come."

Her body shook at his words, her mouth demanding more from his as she ground her pussy further into is palm. Heat skittered across her belly as Damen curled fingers deeper, the force driving her toward the edge.

Sliding his hand from her neck, he cupped her full breast, kneading her stiff bare nipple. He pinched the hard peak and Henley tore her mouth from his, panting.

"Oh my God, *Damen!*"

"What, love?" His lips slid into a sly grin before he broke their kiss to dip his head and bite her nipple. "Is there something you want?"

"Your mouth on my clit!"

Damen pulled his hand from between her legs and licked her slickness from his fingers one at a time, moaning at the taste of her. "Juicy and sweet. Oh, babe. My cock is throbbing. I'm gonna have blue balls before this night is out."

A broken smirk tugged at his lips and he let his hands slide over her thighs to her knees, pushing them wide. He growled at the glistening flesh of her slick, bare mound. "Good enough to eat."

She reached for the button on his pants, but he shook his head. "Tonight's all about you." He smiled angling his head as he crouched low. His tongue flicked her wet nub, and he nodded. "Your taste is on my tongue and on my hands, love. I'll rub one off later thinking about your pretty pink pussy, but right now, I'm not done savoring you."

Damen dipped his head to her pussy and lapped at her lips, his tongue rasping across the sensitive flesh of her tight bud. Henley's head dropped back against the cushions as he licked and sucked. His teeth grazed her swollen flesh as his fingers curled into her wet slit, working her hard. She hissed as he bit her clit, but her entire body tensed as he pulled the taut nub deep into his mouth.

She gasped, holding her breath as he plunged deeper, sucking and working her body as she lifted her hips, grinding for more. Her body tensed, cresting higher and higher until she cried out, her climax exploding, ripping through her body.

Damen pressed his fingers deeper, holding her tightly as she rode the apex to the end. He pulled his fingers from her, licking them clean before sitting back.

SEVEN

"You look amazing," he said slipping onto the couch beside her flushed body. "I could watch you come like that every day." He slid his arm around her naked shoulders letting her slump against his chest.

"It would never work. Not unless I plan to never walk again," she joked.

Dragging in a breath, she sat back to look at him. "Would it break triad rules for me to lend a helping hand here?" Her fingers drifted to the bulge at his crotch. "It's a pretty big package. Might be too *hard* to handle alone."

His eyes darkened and he leaned in to kiss her mouth. "If I have my way one day my big package will handle you *hard* every way it can."

She gasped against his lips and undid the top button of his jeans, but before she could guide the zipper down, he circled her wrist and shook his head. "In time, Hen." He gently pushed her hand away and then bent to grab her clothes from the floor. "The bathroom is over there." He gestured to the back. "Why not take a hot bath? Ivy and Riley are probably wondering where you are, plus I've got to finish getting ready. It'll be morning before I know it." He put her clothes on the couch. "Take your time."

Taking her clothes, she got up from the couch and walked to the bathroom, watching him as he went back to packing. The whole apartment was dim, so she snapped on the light and stood in the backlight.

"Damen?"

He looked up from the table strewn with items to be packed.

She cupped both breasts. "If you won't take a helping hand, I will."

He dropped whatever was in his hand and was at the bathroom door in two strides. Resting his hands on either side of the doorjamb, he leaned in to take her mouth, but she dropped to her knees, dragging her hands over his belly.

"Henley—*no*," he tried again.

Before he could stop her, she finished what she started earlier and unzipped his pants, pulling them past his thighs. His cock jutted long and hard, and she wrapped her hand around its corded shaft, grazing its velvet head with her thumb.

"Henley," he ground out. "I can't."

She shook her head, her eyes on his as they darkened with need. "You may call all the shots when it comes to securing this castle, Iceri, but when it comes to playtime, I don't play like that. I play like this—" Henley dipped her mouth to his engorged head and ringed its ridged underside with the tip of her tongue before sucking his cock between her lips.

He groaned watching his dick disappeared down her throat, his breath hitching as she milked his shaft.

"Oh, fuck. Yes!" His fingers slipped from the sides of the door to fist her hair. He pumped his cock, sliding in and out between her lips, each time driving deeper.

Her hand came up to cup his balls, and she caressed the soft flesh as her opposite palm stroked the length of his shaft as it slipped in and out of her mouth.

Damen groaned, licking his lips. "Harder, baby. Run your palm over my head." She did what he asked and he sucked a breath through his teeth. "Holy fuck," he groaned. "Your mouth is so hot, so good. Faster. *Mmmm*.

71

Harder. Suck me deep."

A low rumble from his throat had her picking up her pace, his thigh muscles clenching and his ass tightened. "So fucking sexy. Your tongue and your lips wrapped around my dick."

Henley inhaled, her eyes going wide as his engorged head swelled even more. Damen thrust his hips, pushing his member to the back of her throat, plunging deeper and faster until he held still before sliding his length from her mouth.

He wrapped his hand around his shaft. "Tongue my balls and work my length with your hand."

Henley's hand covered his and together they worked his cock. Damen hissed, sucking a breath through his teeth. "Oh, baby, I'm so close. Open your mouth and take all of me."

Henley ran her tongue up the corded base of his cock and then sucked his head between her lips. Letting her teeth graze his sensitive flesh, in and out. Damen's entire body went stiff and his dick flexed, rigid in her hand. "I want you to swallow everything I give you."

He pulled his cock from her mouth and held it, working his shaft over her outstretched tongue. With a guttural growl, a hot burst shot from his dick to her mouth, and he held tightly, milking every last drop.

Henley wiped her mouth on the back of her hand and looked up at Damen's scrunched face as aftershocks rocked his body. She straightened, pulling him with her into the bathroom.

"Since we're going to hell for breaking the rules, how about a hot bath to get used to the heat?" she teased.

He nodded, his eyes dark and unfathomable, with red streaks invading the deep chocolate. "Hot wants what hot gets, and hot is what you are, love, but we didn't break the rules. Not technically anyway. I didn't mate."

"So, if we didn't break the rules, then let me come with you." She slipped a hand around his waist as his cock thickened against her belly again.

He met her grin with one of his own. "You don't take no for an answer, do you?"

"Nope." She grinned. "So? Yes?"

He shook his head. "Next time." He walked with her backward, farther into the bathroom. "And speaking of a next time—" He scooped her onto the edge of the granite vanity and buried his face in her pussy.

* * *

"Are we cleared for launch?" Jag asked,

poking his head through the transport bridge door.

Monitors blinked in the background as coordinates scrolled in fast. The pilot pushed the side of his headset back and nodded. "Two minutes. Best secure whatever is left in the cabin. Weather forecasts indicate turbulence ahead the closer we get to the Mirror Mountain peaks."

Jag nodded and closed the bridge door behind him. He turned, watching Damen lock the last of the overhead storage bins. "All set?"

"Yes. That was the last of it." He sat in his seat and fastened his belt. "I figured the least I could do was bring delicacies from the capital. Maybe Gunnar won't be as foul as I expect."

Jag smirked, chuckling. "Well, you brought enough to feed an army."

"Just as well, because for this trip we might end up needing one." Damen inhaled, glancing out the oval transport window. "Looks clear. Maybe we won't get that turbulence after all."

Jag shrugged. "Maybe."

"Launch in thirty seconds. Securing transport doors," the pilot's voice announced over the cabin speakers. "Arrival set, zero six hundred hours."

Damen waggled his eyebrows. "Like Henley says, buckle up, baby."

Jag's eyes narrowed for a moment and then he burst out laughing. "You dog! You dirty dog! Riley said Hen didn't come back after she left the royal apartment."

"That's Mr. Dirty Dog to you, sir." Damen shrugged. "I'm a hungry bear and Henley had exactly what I craved."

The cabin shook as the transport revved for launch. The engines burned and ignition sent the shuttle out the bay doors, the small craft gaining altitude quickly before leveling off.

"Sure beats horseback, that's for sure. That desert heat is no joke and we've already crossed the sand to the base of the mountain twice this year," Damen continued.

Jag exhaled. "Don't remind me. At least this time we're not chasing one of our women. Is it me or are they all hard headed? Ivy, Riley and especially that tall drink of water you got busy with last night."

"Hey! Not nice. Henley may be stubborn, but she's no fool, and as for getting busy, that's none of your business," Damen shot back.

Jag snorted. "Dude, your face. Either you've got motion sickness, or I hit a nerve." He lifted a hand. "Listen, I don't blame you. Henley is something else. She's feisty and strong, but she cares and is fiercely loyal. It's like she's got the best of Ivy and Riley plus her own fire."

"Tell me about it." Damen smirked "That fire nearly burned me to a crisp last night and that's all I'm gonna say."

Jag looked at him, concerned. "What about Gunnar? He's not going to be too happy when he hears."

"I didn't break the triad compact. Came damn close, but everything between alpha and omega is still intact." He shrugged. "Besides, it's not like he's ever going to set eyes on Henley, so what would be the point? My hands are tied, Jag. You know that."

The cabin shook, juddering and listing to one side. "Turbulence boys! As promised. Hang on!" the pilot's voice crackled.

"Shit! Maybe horseback was the better choice after all!" Jag chuckled, gripping the arms to his seat.

"Ouch! Damn! Help!" a muffled female voice yelled from somewhere. "Can anyone hear me? Ugh! I'm gonna be sick!"

Damen exchanged looks with Jag and they both unbuckled their seatbelts and held on as best they could as they knocked on the inner storage compartments. "Hello! Is anyone there?" Jag called.

"Here! I'm in here! Help!"

Damen's eyes narrowed. "It can't be."

"Keep talking!" Jag shouted as the two men stumbled, holding onto to whatever was bolted down.

Jag pointed to a tall narrow compartment and reaching with one hand, undid the latch. Henley tumbled out, landing on her side like a spilled sack of potatoes.

"Well, so much for Gunnar never setting eyes on her," Jag teased.

Damen moved to her side pitching forward as the transport lurched again. "I should've known. Henley, what the hell are you doing here? I told you the trip was off limits!"

Jag managed to get back in his seat. He clasped his belt and locked the clip, motioning for Damen to do the same. "You can interrogate her later. The turbulence is getting worse. Look outside. We're flying through a blizzard! Buckle up or you'll both be knocked out."

Scowling, Damen dragged her into a chair and fastened her belt before doing the same for himself. "Of all the stupid, headstrong, unthinking things to do!" He glared at her. "You could have suffocated in there or frozen to death!"

"I...I...didn't think."

He raked a hand through his dark hair. "No,

77

you didn't. I know I joked last night with you not taking no for an answer, but damn it, Henley. You could have really been hurt! Not to mention we are headed into hostile territory. It's fucking cold where we're going and you're in a tee-shirt and leggings."

She lifted her chin. "It's long sleeved and I'm wearing boots, plus I brought a jacket. It's in the...the...thing." She gestured to the storage compartment.

"The hold?" Damen replied. "Where we store goods and equipment. The hold that isn't pressurized for living beings?"

"Okay, okay —" She winced. "I get it. Stupid stowaway move, but there was no way I was spending one more day as part of the baby central. I need this, Damen." She raised an eyebrow. "Remember *need*?"

He stared at her, but his eyes darkened for a moment and a smirk tugged at his lips.

"Besides, I thought a lot about what you said last night about this alpha guy. If I'm not a one-night stand, then maybe that means I'm supposed to be something else to you." She looked at him, encouraging. "It's worth finding out, right? It's like you told Jag, your alpha/omega thing is intact."

He frowned. "Eavesdropping is not nice."

"It's not like I could help it, besides you were very gallant." She smiled. "Most guys would kiss and tell after the night we had."

Jag stuck his fingers in his ears. "Okay...*lalalalalala*. Riley's not here to take the edge off and I can't walk around torqued up for however long this expedition lasts, so you two need to cork it!"

"We're through the turbulence, but conditions at the hover site are too dangerous between the peaks. We're going to have to drop you on the opposite side. I hope you packed warm," the pilot announced. "Ten minutes."

"Hover site?" Henley asked.

Jag nodded. "The shuttle can't land outside a transport bay, so we have to jump."

"Jump." She looked from one to the other. "Like we did with Gerri when we came to Nova?"

Damen shook his head. "Ever been extreme skiing?"

EIGHT

The inner transport door slid open and an icy blast blew through the inside cabin. Heavy wind rocked the craft as Jag tossed the last of their belongings out the egress. He then slipped a small backpack over his shoulders, tossing a second one to Damen.

"Wait, what are you doing?" she asked as Damen stepped behind her, taking her arms.

"It's like a parachute. I don't need one, so you can use mine," he said, slipping the wide straps up and over her shoulders.

Jag pointed out the opening and then tapped his wrist. We have to go. The shuttle can't hover much longer in this wind."

Eyes wide, she looked between the two, incredulous. "You want me to jump alone? On Earth, people never jump alone the first time.

Can't we do it together?" she asked, yelling over the din of the wind.

Damen looked down at her with a smirk. "Isn't that the whole point of you tagging along? So that we can *do it* together?"

"Hey, hey…what did I say about corking it?" Jag teased. "Just put on the damn chute, Damen, and drop with her. She's not that big."

Henley burst out laughing. "Now that's something I've heard before, like never!"

"You guys need to go, now or I have to abort!" the pilot crackled over the loud speaker.

Damen yanked the pack from Henley's shoulders and quickly fastened it on himself. "Wrap your legs around my waist and hold on tight!"

She jumped up, hiking her legs and arms as he said and with a yell, Damen dove from the transport with Jag right behind.

"Don't kill us, you big bear!" she ground out, hiding her face in his neck. Adrenaline poured into her blood making her skin vibrate with excitement. This was fucking amazing!

The wind whipped at them as they freefell. Henley held with a death grip as Damen whooped, hollering as they dove. He pulled the string last minute and they floated to the snowy embankment.

"You can let go, now," he joked, chuckling as she gripped his neck.

"That was incredible!" She sucked in a breath and let go, putting one leg down and then the other. There was almost no wind on the ridge and she turned, still in his arms, pushing her hair from her face. The views stunned her for a moment, locking her breath in her throat as she took in the landscape. "Forget the dive! Damen…*this* is amazing!"

"No, you stubborn, reckless remarkable girl. You are the one who's amazing," he whispered, leaning down to kiss her hair. "No woman I know is as brave."

He sounded almost proud, and she felt herself blush. "So, I'm no longer rash and unthinking?"

"Nope. That, you are." He let go of her waist to help Jag with the supplies. "But you're also wild and uninhibited and I wouldn't change that about you for the world."

She stifled a sigh, turning instead to the vista ahead. Inhaling the clean, crisp air she nodded to herself. "So this is where you grew up."

Now she understood why the majestic peaks were called the Mirror Mountains. They were the complete mirror image of each other. Opposite but equal, and just as imposing. Her breath puffed out in white clouds, but she wasn't cold. She was exhilarated.

"Not quite," Damen replied lifting one of the heavy packing containers he brought for his clan and stowing it under a rock overhang. "I grew up on the opposite side of this ridge. The Summit clan likes its privacy, and the gorge between the Mirror peaks provides that."

She looked at him as he and Jag lifted and carried. Privacy or isolation? Her guess was isolation.

"Can I help?" she asked making a muscle. "I'm pretty strong for a chick."

Jag rolled his eyes. "It's bad enough you stowed away in the first place. If you get hurt lugging this stuff, there's no way to get you back to the Palladia. In case you hadn't noticed, we're in the middle of frozen Nomadville. As it is, you're going to stay with Damen's clan while we head into the jungle. That's if they let us stay. In the meantime, we need to get these supplies hidden. There are rogue elements on this mountain."

"Watch your mouth, Kasaval, or we'll watch as you freeze your royal ass stuck out on this ridge."

Damen stopped mid-lug and turned toward the voice. He hoisted the container from his shoulder and placed it beside him in the snow. Jag walked to his side and Henley scooted closer as five men crested a far snowdrift.

They stopped twenty feet from where the three of them stood. Four men flanked the one at the center, two on each side. They were as big as any other Galaxan male, but rougher. Almost brutal in their furs and skins.

"Not all mountain men are rogues, Your Highness, although some of us *are* deserters," the man at the center of the greeting party said.

Henley's gaze settled on the man. His voice was like steel and silk. Hard and cold, yet smooth and sensual. He was gorgeous with blond scruff on a chiseled jaw. Bright blue eyes missed nothing, and the sleek fur hat on his head made him seem even more rugged and sexy. He stepped forward and slid a fur-lined glove from his hand, extending it to Jag.

"The Summit Clan welcomes you," he said, clearly ignoring Damen.

Henley raised an eyebrow, but when the man pulled his hat from his head, she sucked in a breath. Like the Mirror Mountains on either side of them, the man standing opposite Jag might as well have been the mirror image of Damen. Opposite but alike. Light where Damen was dark.

Gunnar.

MILLY TAIDEN

There was no other explanation that fit.

Jag took the man's hand, yet Damen's face was a mask. Henley slipped her hand into his, noting the shadow crossing his eyes.

"Gunnar. I didn't expect you to greet us, considering," Damen said.

The mountain alpha looked at Damen, his gaze cold. "Considering what? That you ran out on our clan? Abandoned your end of our contract?" Blue eyes slid toward Henley and they flicked from her face downward and then back. He inhaled, his gaze tightening. "Your latest conquest, Damen? I didn't expect you to return after all this time with your hat in hand, but I didn't expect disrespect. I guess I should have known better."

Henley looked at Damen, ignoring his nearly imperceptible warning. "Excuse me? I understand you two have unfinished business, but don't for one second think you can use me as a weapon in this testosterone-driven standoff. What I am to Damen is none of your business, and I resent the implication that my presence is disrespectful. You don't know me, yet you have no problems hurling insults my way.

"As for Damen, he at least greeted you with civility, which is more than I can say for the way you've treated us. You're the alpha of your clan? Well, maybe you should learn to lead by example.

You want respect, then you need to learn to show respect. In the meantime, you want to have a pissing contest with Damen, go right ahead. Whatever floats your boat, but leave me out of it. When the two of you decide to play nice in this frozen sandbox, then come talk to me. Until that time, I'm Switzerland." She dragged a level hand in front of her chest.

Blue eyes flashed, but a smirk tugged at the gorgeous line of Gunnar's mouth. "Switzerland?"

"It's a country back home on Earth famous for its neutrality," she replied.

Gunnar nodded, sparing a glance for Damen. "I can see the attraction, brother. She's got fire in her belly like a Summit woman."

Jag took the man's hand and shook it. "Thank you for the welcome, Gunnar. I suppose you received Vander's communique about our arrival."

"Yes, I received it via satellite yesterday. I have rooms ready, if you'll follow us." He let go of Jag's hand and as he turned his eyes moved to the supply bins under the rocky overhang. "If there's anything of value in those we need to take them now, if not, can I send men back for them later?"

Damen stepped forward. "They are for the clan. Fine fabrics and thread, dried fruits and nuts, chocolate and sweets for the children and, of course, cases of Sidaii." His dark eyes met Gunnar's blue. "I brought them as peace offerings, Gunnar. Whatever you think of me, I have never forgotten our people."

He hmmphed in reply. "Really. Considering you never answered one of my communiques, I find that hard to believe."

"What communiques? I never received a single message, Gunnar. Your last words to me were that I was shunned. I didn't question your silence because Cero banned contact with me." He paused, raising an eyebrow. "Since when does the Summit have transmission technology for communiques?"

Gunnar eyed him, his blue gaze somber. "A lot has changed since you left, Damen. You would have known had you answered my communiques."

"How could I reply when none of your messages reached me? If they were sent at all," he scoffed.

Jag got between the two and their escalating argument. "How about we continue this debate in a place where I won't freeze my balls? I've got a mate who'd like me to father her children at some point."

Henley snickered at that, stifling a shiver.

Her coat left with the shuttle.

Gunnar didn't miss a beat. He pulled his coat from his back and slipped it over Henley's shoulders. His fingers lingered for just a second, but in that moment, she was very much aware of the man and his touch. His scent surrounded her, mingling with Damen's from before and her hand moved to her stomach and the butterflies winging around at top speed.

Maybe Gerri was wrong, and she was a ho. Damen had rocked her world with his tongue buried in her pussy less than twenty-four hours ago, and here she was with her nether regions buzzing for a hot blonde. Gunnar was the equal and opposite member of a future triad along with Damen. She shivered at the thought of them both together with her. Maybe a dirty threesome wasn't such a strange idea after all.

Gunnar's blue gaze found her hazel eyes and locked for a moment. His nostrils flared, and she waited for them to narrow knowing he could scent Damen on her from the night before, but they didn't. His eyes changed slightly, the color darkening to almost a navy blue and he pulled his gaze from hers to find Damen as he watched.

Neither said a word, but something was exchanged, she was sure. Gunnar pulled his fingers from her shoulders, leaving his fur behind. He spared a nod to his omega, and in that moment, Damen's body language changed. Almost as if whatever was between them was settled, or at least on the mend.

Damen walked beside Gunnar, and Henley hurried to slide in next to Jag as the others carried the supplies. "Is it my imagination, or did things just change?" she whispered.

"Something changed. Maybe Gunnar decided not to kill Damen after all," Jag replied.

She stared at the prince, her mouth hanging open and her throat suddenly tight. "Holy crap! Was that even a possibility? Why the hell did Vander let him come, then?"

"At first, he wasn't going to let him." Jag looked at her, almost gauging how much to say. "I was originally doing this as a solo. Vander knew Gunnar would agree to help if the request came by royal appeal, but there was a distinct possibility he'd tell us to shit in a hat if Damen showed his face. To be honest, it was Gerri who convinced Vander to let Damen accompany me." He shrugged. "She's small, but she's mighty and we've learned not to underestimate her when she calls a spade a spade."

Henley's brows knotted and she looked at the two hulking men walking ten feet ahead. One light. One dark. But mirror images nonetheless. Damen's words came back.

My hands are tied, Henley.

I can't. Not solo, anyway.

I'm part of a triad…

She watched the two of them together and how their bodies moved alike, sexy, like predators in motion. Sensual. Carnal. Butterflies kamikazed in her stomach.

"Gerri Wilder. You are one sneaky, old wench," she muttered to herself.

NINE

Damen stopped under the wide stone arch that led through to the Summit village. His eyes took in every stone, every building, before looking for Gunnar.

"I told you, much has changed since you left," the alpha replied to the omega's quiet appraisal.

Damen raised an eyebrow. "How did you get Cero to agree to join the progressive age? You've got communication towers and holographic transmitters between our traditional stone and wood buildings," he said. "When? How?"

"After you left. Cero tried to keep his hold on the council. They never expected you to call the old man's bluff. To be honest, neither did I." He shrugged. "When we discovered you gone the next morning, there was hell to pay. The elder council blamed Cero," Gunnar paused. "And me."

Damen spared Gunnar and doubtful look. "You? You're their golden child, literally," he said moving his hand up and down.

"Fat lot it did me without you here." Gunnar walked through the arched gateway and motioned to his men. "Bring the supplies and the gifts from the capital to the main hall. We can set them up for distribution later."

Henley and Jag walked up, stopping beside Damen at the gate. Gunnar turned, sweeping his arm toward a massive chalet carved into the side of the mountain and the picturesque homes and shops along the snowy road that winded upward to the lodge.

"This is Summit. Welcome," he said with a smile, and turning to Damen he inclined his head, but didn't offer more. "Rooms are prepared." He slid his eyes to Henley. "I'll have to make arrangements for you, though, love. I didn't know Damen was bringing company."

She lifted her chin. "Now, now. I thought I asked not to be a pawn in your pissing match…and you two were behaving so nicely too." She clicked the inside of her cheek.

"My apologies," he replied with a smirk. "Still, I wish I had known you were accompanying the expedition."

Damen nodded moving to Henley's side. "Yeah, you and me both. She's a stowaway. Her adventure junkie got the better of her and she snuck onto the transport and fell out of a storage hold when we hit turbulence."

Gunnar's lips spread in a wide appreciative grin. "Fire."

"Yeah, well. If you two don't fix what's wrong between you, I might have to burn you both for the hell of it," she huffed, pushing past them on the path.

Both Gunnar and Damen burst out laughing and she glanced over her shoulder, catching a glimpse of what the two must have been like as teenagers, before their elders interfered. Her heart squeezed. Maybe Gerri was right and Damen needed to be here.

"Well, are you going to stand there staring or are you going to show me around? This place is a winter wonderland, and since I'm Switzerland for the next week or so, I declare this neutral territory, just like me," she flashed them a smile and together they shook their heads. "Chop, chop, boys. Mama's hungry and she wants to sightsee before we hit the big bad jungle."

Gunnar's eyes flew to Damen. "You're not seriously letting her come with us to find the

Hatun? You know what lurks in the shadows that far in, or have you forgotten that as well?"

Damen stepped closer, stiff-jawed. "My memory is perfect, and no, she's not coming with us."

The two stared at each other for a moment, mouths tight.

"Good. At least you haven't lost what sense the gods gave you," Gunnar replied, but before Damen could shoot back, she got between them.

"Enough. Please," Henley argued. "I know you two have a lot to talk about, but can't it wait until we're in front of a fire or something? Or at least until I can feel my feet again? Whatever adrenaline I had from jumping out of that transport is gone. My hands, feet, and nose are about to shatter, they're so cold."

Gunnar didn't wait. He scooped her up in his arms and started up the path.

"Hey!" she cried. "I can walk myself!" She squirmed against his rock hard chest, but all that did was make him chuckle.

The soft rumble and the way he smelled up close and personal sent her libido into orbit. He was as intoxicating as Damen. And the two were supposed to be a matched set? Holy hotness and damp panties!

Jag and Damen flanked Gunnar as they

trekked toward the chalet. She peeked at Damen over Gunnar's huge shoulder, blowing the fur from his coat away from her face.

"Stop smirking, bear boy. I know what you're thinking," she mumbled.

Damen's grin went ear to ear and her eyes went wide that he heard her and Gunnar chuckled even more at the way she stiffened. "He's a shifter, Henley, of course he heard you. I'll let you in on a trade secret. He knows what you're thinking, too." He slid his eyes to hers, a soft smirk on his lips as her cheeks flushed against his hard chest. "And so do I."

She wanted to crawl under the nearest rock, but she settled for hiding her face in his shoulder. The hike up the long winding path didn't bother her so much once she got over her embarrassment. Of course, Gunnar and Damen were tuned in. They were a pair. Plus, it didn't help her libido announced every dirty thought that crossed her mind.

She squashed the images and focused on the scenery. Smoke curled from quaint wood and stone cabins dotting the path to the chalet, and she sighed.

"Do you like my home?" Gunnar asked.

Henley nodded. "It looks like it belongs in a storybook."

"It does indeed." He paused. "It's one of the reasons we tried to keep ourselves isolated. Look at what's happening in the capital. If you stay small and secluded, no evil touches you."

She picked her head up, taking in the hard line of his gorgeous jaw. "You don't believe that, though. Otherwise you wouldn't have modernized your communications systems and some of your infrastructure."

"I did what I had to, Henley. It doesn't mean I like it."

She angled her head, watching him. "This place looks like a storybook, and right now you look like a character I know. Pinocchio. His nose would grow whenever he told a lie." She reached out and tapped the end of Gunnar's nose. "Tweet, tweet. Birds are gonna perch on yours soon."

He rolled his eyes, but when his gaze settled on her, she nearly choked on her tongue at desire in their blue depths.

"Fire and intelligence wrapped in soft delicious curves. No wonder my brother omega found you irresistible," he murmured.

She cleared her throat. "Uhm, I'm not so sure about that. I stowed away, remember? It's not like I gave him much choice."

"And if he gave you a choice. One that opened our storybook to you with us as your

Prince Charmings? What about then?" Gunnar turned to look at her, their faces only inches apart.

She wanted to kiss him as badly as she had wanted to kiss Damen. Just one taste. Damen didn't need to know. Then again, with the way the two were fighting, it could cause a world war. Or maybe not. Maybe wanting them both was a way to get them to talk. The blue of Gunnar's eyes held her mesmerized, and as if he'd read her mind, he brought his head down and brushed his lips softly over hers.

Bursts rocketed in her chest. She moaned into the kiss and Gunnar deepened it, swiping his tongue into her mouth to caress hers. She raised her free hand to his face, his scruff adding to the visceral pleasure. His kiss was rough, almost primal in the same way that Damen's was full and demanding, but they both held a kind of desperation. As if they had no choice but to hold back.

He pulled her closer to his chest, deepening their kiss. Tightness coiled in her belly as images of Damen and Gunnar together flooded her mind. Moisture pooled in her panties and she gasped as he slipped a hand beneath the coat he lent to cup her breast, teasing her nipple through her long sleeve tee. She closed her eyes and her clit throbbed with the need to come.

"Has Damen had you," he murmured

against her lips.

She froze for a moment. Was this just about rivalry or was he asking because Damen was his omega and with her here there was a chance for their triad to be complete?

"I smell him on you, Henley, but my own senses are fogged with want. I don't trust my wits. Are you the one? Is that why you're here?" he asked, his voice a low rasp.

Her tongue traced his bottom lip and she shook her head. "Damen made it all about me, and I made it all about him in return. Separately. I don't know if that answers your question."

"It does." His lips curled in a smile. "So he's still my omega, then...and you?"

She pulled back, breaking what was left of their moment to look at him. "I think you need to square things with Damen before anything else. Why don't you focus on that first?"

"Gunnar," Jag said, "you, Damen, and I need to meet to plan a strategy on how best to locate and destroy the Unduru. Whether that means involving the Hatun or not, I don't know."

She and Gunnar both looked at the two men walking slightly behind, and Henley's eyes caught Damen's and for a moment he looked conflicted. She winked, blowing him a kiss and he smiled.

"We can meet in my study once you're settled and had a chance to eat and rest. We've got the entire evening to talk." His eyes met Damen's as well. "There is much to discuss."

TEN

Henley closed the door behind her, dragging in a quick breath. She didn't know which was worse, the women at the chalet with their curious stares, or the ones peeking through the windows as Gunnar carried her all the way to his front door.

She hadn't felt that self-conscious since college. She put her backpack on a chair and then exhaled. The accommodations Gunnar provided were enormous with an expansive bed and the biggest fireplace she'd seen crackling away with fragrant pine and herbs.

The windows overlooked the mountains and she moved the sheer curtains aside to looked at the gorgeous vistas beyond the picturesque village. The snow had a definite pink tone, but then again that might have been an illusion from the dual suns as they set. It was nearly twilight and she wondered what Ivy and Riley were doing. And if Vander had busted a gut when he found out she had stowed away.

Too late now, unless the king sent another transport ordering her back to the Palladian capital. She shook her head watching the pinks and golds sparkle on the snowy roofs. A knock on the door had her turning, and the door opened halfway.

A tall, slender woman with long white-gray hair smiled from the entry. "May I come in?" she asked. In her arms were layers of clothing in bright, cheerful colors.

Henley nodded and the woman stepped through, closing the door once more. She turned with a smile, gesturing with her bundle. "I brought a few of my outfits. We don't have armoires that conjure clothes at a mere wish…not yet, anyway." She smiled. "Gunnar isn't quite there yet, but we're working on him."

"We're?" Henley asked.

The woman nodded. "My daughters and I. I'm Marta, Gunnar and Damen's *Aegis*."

"Their guardian? Aren't they a little old to be considered wards?" Henley asked raising an eyebrow.

Marta laughed, putting the garments on the large bed. "Of course, they are, still…I can't help remembering them as boys together." She nodded. "I help run Gunnar's house. With Damen gone for so long, there's been no—" she cut her words, dropping her eyes to her hands for a moment. "That is to say, neither of my boys have found their mate…yet." The awkward moment faded, and she looked at Henley with a soft smile. "Thank you for bringing Damen home. For the first time, the Summit clan has hope."

"Wait, I didn't bring Damen home." Henley shook her head. "He was coming home anyway, I just invited myself along."

Marta gave her a knowing look. "Everything happens for a reason, dear." With a nod, she turned to the bed and the pretty garments she put on the thick coverlet. "There are dresses and pants sets for you to choose from. I wasn't sure which you'd be more comfortable wearing. Each is warm and trimmed with fur. They should help you acclimate."

"Acclimate?" Henley asked.

Marta nodded. "To the cold."

"Oh, yeah. That." Henley bobbed her head. "Thanks."

The older woman turned on her heel but stopped, gesturing toward the door on the opposite side of the room. "The bathroom has everything you'll need in the cabinet. Find me if you need anything else."

"Thank you. I think I'll take a shower and then get something to eat. Is there a kitchen somewhere I could raid?" Henley asked with a smile.

Marta waved one hand. "I'll see to that. Gunnar gave orders you were to have whatever you want."

The older woman left, shutting the door behind her and Henley went to the window again. The Summit was truly something out of a fairytale. If she only liked the cold.

She smirked, watching the smoke curl from the chimneys before turning to the crackling fire in the room's hearth. "Girl, who'd be cold, snuggled in front of a fire with two of the hottest men in the universe?"

"My question exactly."

Henley's eyes jerked to the door. "Damen…I didn't hear you come in."

"I wanted to make sure you got settled," he said closing the distance between them in two strides. His lips found hers and she sighed, sinking into the familiar taste of him.

She sighed, but he broke their kiss before she could even slide her fingers into his hair. "Wow, that was pretty cheap."

"Cheap?" He grinned. "You didn't look like you thought a simple kiss cheap when brother bigfoot carried you most of the way here."

She giggled. "Not nice, Damen. In fact, you sound jealous."

"I'm not, really." He shrugged. "I guess I'm not used to sharing anymore, but then again, if Gunnar's inner bear wants you as much as I do, we could have lift off, if you know what I mean."

Damen waggled his eyebrows and she laughed, letting her eyes dip to the bulge behind his zipper. "Lift off? That thing looks like it's ready to blow now."

"Baby, you have no idea." He gathered her in his arms again. "I'd ask if you care to say *ah* again, but I've got to meet Jag and Gunnar downstairs. Maybe later?" He nodded with an expectant grin.

She turned him around and pushed him toward the door. "Go. Have your meeting, and we'll see about later. In the meantime, I'm going to take a nap and then a maybe a quick shower before I go in search of food."

"I thought Marta was sending you up a tray," he said with his hand on the doorknob. "I'll make sure she sends it up now so you're not disturbed later." He glanced at the clothes on the bed. "That woman was always relentless." He chuckled. "Kind of like someone else I know."

He left with a wink, leaving her with a smirk on her lips. Henley turned, her eyes taking in the expansive bed across from the fireplace.

Big enough for three.

She smoothed the front of her hair, winding her long ponytail around her fingers. What was this? France? Ménage a trois was not something she went looking for.

Then again…

"Ugh…your brain is turning into a walking talking porn show." She peeled off her coat and tossed it onto the chair before picking up her pack and emptying the contents on the bed. She shook her head at the items she packed. Leggings and tank tops, tees, sneakers, underwear and toiletries including combination bug spray and sunscreen.

"You packed for tropical and you got tundra." Shaking her head again she shoved everything back in the pack and put it on the chair again.

She lifted a crimson tunic top trimmed in black fur. The material was like nothing she'd felt before. Soft, but with a generous give. There were matching pants that looked as if they would be as comfortable as her leggings. Henley moved to the closet to hang up the garments Marta was kind enough to offer, then she noticed a gorgeous robe, white silk, trimmed with the softest lace.

Stripping, she folded her clothes and put them and her backpack in the bottom of the closet. She closed the door and then dove for the bed, snuggling into the soft covers. The guys would be strategizing for hours. She could catch a quick nap, have something to eat and then shower just in case Damen decided to come by as promised. She smirked in anticipation, sitting up at another knock on the door.

"Come in," she said, swinging bare legs over the edge of the mattress.

A girl backed into the room with a large serving tray, and Henley jumped up to help.

"It's okay, miss. I'm used to carrying heavy trays. Gunnar eats like a bear, and he's always hungry." She giggled giving Henley a shy smile before putting the tray on the coffee table in the room's sitting area. "Call when you want me to come and collect it."

The girl left and Henley stared after her. Gunnar's always hungry? If that giggle meant what she thought it meant, then the alpha wasn't that different from his omega when it came to playing poke the bear.

Henley's stomach rumbled and she plopped down on the couch, surveying what Marta sent up. The tray was packed with every kind of food she could want. Roast chicken and fresh rolls and butter, loaded baked potatoes, biscuits and gravy, fruit and cakes. She made herself a plate and then curled her legs under, watching the snow fall.

As she ate, she noticed a bottle of Sidaii wine and three glasses were on the room's sideboard. "Well, who am I to upset their matchmaking plans," she said to herself before getting up to pour a glass. She half expected a note from Gerri scrawled with the theme song from the TV show Three's Company. Subtle was not the woman's strong suit.

She sipped her wine, picking at what was left on her plate. Gunnar and Damen. You couldn't dream up two more perfect men. Still, at least she knew Damen. She'd been half in love with the man since they arrived on Galaxa, but Gunnar? She just met the gorgeous bear of a man and already he occupied her thoughts like no one's business. The man didn't crowd out Damen from her mind. Just the opposite. And that kiss….

That absolutely amazing kiss.

Her cheeks flushed and she reached into the wine bucket for a handful of ice. Holding it to her neck, she let the cold, melted water drip between her breasts. She closed her eyes imagining both men and their talented mouths on her body, her lips, her breasts.

Her eyes snapped open and she dropped

what was left of the ice on the tray. This was crazy. She was hot and bothered over both men. Literally. Truth was she didn't have to be. It's not like they were in competition with each other. They had the same goal. Her. At least that's what she thought.

What if she was wrong and they didn't want her for their triad?

What if she was just their plaything du jour?

She got up to glance out the window again, wondering. Draining her glass, she climbed onto the bed again and curled into one of the soft pillows. She'd find out soon enough...or not.

ELEVEN

"We either take the highland trail to the bottom of the northern Mirror and then cross the river to the base of the southern steppes or we send Vander a communique that we need a hover transport. Either way we can't get to the edge of the Tempera jungle from here without mountain hopping," Jag tapped the map. "If we take the highland trail, it will be three days at least before we get to the bottom of the northern slope. Then another day at least to cross over to the southern side."

Gunnar leaned on his desk, folding his arms across his chest. "If Vander sends a hover transport it could drop us right to the base, but then we lose the element of surprise."

"Do you really thing the Hatun won't see us coming the minute we cross into their territory?" Damen pointed out, trying his best not to antagonize Gunnar. Their entire conversation had been like walking on eggshells, but he had light years more experience at this. "Those vines have eyes, not to mention the northern mountain rogues who trade with the Hatun. They'll give them a heads up before we even cross the river onto the southern slope. Either way, we're up against it. At least with a hover transport we're not wasting time."

Gunnar pushed himself away from the desk and moved to his sideboard. He poured three glasses of clear liquid and handed one to each of the guys. He tipped the edge of his glass toward them and winked, taking a sip.

"Ice-wine," Damen said with a grin. "I haven't had this in forever." He lifted the glass to his lips, stifling a moan as the familiar liquid hit his tongue.

Gunnar drained his glass. "If you came home you could have all you want, or if you answered my communiques I could have sent you a bottle or ten."

"I already told you, I never got your messages." Damen dragged a frustrated hand through his dark hair and then looked at his alpha. "How long ago did you start sending them?"

Gunnar shrugged. "Seven or eight years ago. Once I was old enough to take control of the council and started making changes, modernizing. I wanted to tell you, you were right. I wanted you to come home."

Damen blinked, watching Gunnar's face. "What about Cero?" he asked, cautiously.

"It was clear after you left, he wanted to control us. To keep Summit isolated so our people would be too afraid to leave. Make it easy for him to maintain power. After you left, people questioned. They questioned me, not him. I didn't like not having answers for them. At least not answers I believed." He gave his omega a chin pop. "You were right, Damen. I should have stood with you. Not just about joining the rest of the world, but about choosing our mate. No one can do that for us, but us."

Jag watched the interchange. "Uhm, not to interrupt, but I'd have to argue the point. There is one person who could not only find your mate but will hand deliver her to you as well. But if you ask me, I think she's done already that."

Damen smirked and a knowing chuckle rumbled in his chest. "You think Mrs. Wilder put Henley up to stowing away in the transport?"

"Wait, who's this Mrs. Wilder?" Gunnar asked.

Jag jerked a thumb toward the door. "The matchmaker Damen convinced Vander to use to help him find not only his mate, but half the mates for the warriors in the Palladia, including me. She matched me with my mate, Riley. Of course, the beauty of how the woman works is you don't even realize when she manipulates the scenario, and then boom! Too late. You'd rather cut out your heart than live without the girl."

"This Mrs. Wilder, she sent Henley to you?" Gunnar asked.

Damen looked at his alpha, but wasn't sure how to answer. "Not exactly. That's what Jag means. Henley traveled to Galaxa with Riley and Ivy, Vander's mate. She's been at the palace since then, and no matter where I went, she was there. It was as if by design. Since the moment I laid eyes on her, I couldn't get her out of my mind. It's like she's in my blood or something." He eyed Gunnar with a nod. "You felt it. I know you did."

The alpha nodded, raking a hand through his blond mane. "That obvious?"

"Dude, I may have been gone for a long time, but we're still linked. The moment you saw her, took in her scent, I knew. She's not just another pretty face with a luscious body. My animal wants her. My bear that's been asleep for nearly fifteen years is prowling around my gut clawing for release. Clawing to mark her, to claim her."

Gunnar frowned. "She knows you, Damen. For her to stowaway like that, she's probably in love with you. Earth girls are goofy about their feeling from what I hear. They're not dual-natured, so it's all emotion." He shook his head. "Henley will never understand or accept the idea of a triad."

"I already explained it to her. She knew I was coming home, so she knew you'd be here. My gut tells me she's halfway ours already, especially after the way you kissed her this afternoon." His inner bear circled, growling with need at the idea of Henley completing their triad.

"It's not just emotion for Henley. It's physical, too. I feel it. It's been fifteen years since I had to share a woman with anyone, let alone deny myself, but I held back with Henley. The moment my bear stirred, I knew. She's ours, Gunnar. She's meant to complete our triad." Damen drained his glass and the put it on the desk, holding out his hand to the alpha.

The two clasped forearms, brotherhood style. "I hope you're right, dude, because your bear isn't the only one whose dick is as straight as an arrow." Gunnar chuckled, clapping Damen on the back.

Jag lifted his drink and took a sip. "Well, boys, we'll just have to keep her at the Summit until the lady realizes she's got two for the price of one."

Damen stepped back from Gunnar with a

laugh. "Yeah, right. You try and stop her from coming with us into the Tempera. If we want Henley, that means we get her impetuous nature as well."

"Jag, how long will it take Vander to send a hover transport? A day or so?" Gunnar asked.

Jag shrugged. "Probably, why?"

Gunnar shifted his eyes to his omega and nodded. "Two days. Let's show her how good three can be."

* * *

Henley opened her eyes to moonlight shining through the open sheers. She rolled over taking a minute for her eyes to adjust. He mouth felt gritty, and she smacked her lips. Maybe it was the wine.

She must have dozed off longer than she expected. The tray of food was still on the small table in the sitting area, and her empty wine glass on the night table. She swiveled around, letting her legs dangle off the high bed.

She chuckled to herself flexing her feet in the air. "This bed was definitely made for giants."

Getting up, she walked to the window to peer outside. The sky was a gorgeous inky hue, with a carpet of stars like she'd never seen before, not even from the roof of the palace. Voices caught her attention and she turned. Jag was out in the snow covered lawn, playing with a pair of dogs...no wolves. Real wolves or shifter wolves? In a flash, Jag transformed to his ancient cat, and the three took off toward the ice and trees.

Mouth open, she watched them disappear. "Shifters. Definitely."

She turned catching a glimpse of herself in the oval floor mirror beside the armoire. Yikes. Talk about looking like a wild night with none of the fun. She made an about face, grabbed the robe she pulled earlier, and headed straight for the bathroom.

Snapping on the light, she could only stare. "Holy hell," she whispered, pulling the silk material over her. The bath was almost as big as the bedroom suite itself. Polished wood and stone made up the décor, but it was the deep, smooth stone tub that caught her eye most. It looked as if carved from a single slap.

"Now that's a party tub," she stepped closer, kneeling beside the stone rim. "This could hold five people," she murmured to herself with a laugh. "Five regular sized people...or two very large bear shifters and one human girl." She smirked. "Probably takes forever to fill, so mood-kill."

No sooner did the words leave her mouth

than the smooth interior filled with scented, bubbling water. Stunned, she stood with a laugh. "Ha. Like having my own personal hot spring."

"Well, someone as hot as you should have a hot spring," a deep voice said from behind.

Henley whirled, but lost her balance falling backward into the tub. Water sloshed over the edge to the tile floor as she sputtered and coughed. "Damen! Try announcing yourself once in a while, damn it!" she ground out, pushing wet hair from her face.

She hmmphed again, shooting a dirty look toward the door only to see Gunnar standing there instead. Henley blinked, sitting in a soaked robe that clung to her wet breasts, the rest floating around her like a water cloud.

"If you wanted wet," he said walking through wet puddles to the edge of the tub. "I'm sure we could have found other ways."

He held out his hand, and she took it. He helped her to stand, his gaze taking in every inch of her body cased in wet silk.

Vulnerable. That was the first feeling that crept over her, but the heat of Gunnar's eyes squelched the urge to cover up. Instead, she straightened her shoulders and let him look.

Hard nipples peaked beneath the soaked, translucent fabric. Every hollow and curve, highlighted. She lifted her chin and met his intense stare.

"Wow, a private wet tee shirt contest. I should have gotten here sooner." Damen chuckled from the door.

Henley's flicked her gaze to his and watched the humor shift to raw desire. He moved to Gunnar's side and she inhaled, peeling the wet fabric from her shoulders and letting it puddle to the water below her knees.

"Henley—" Damen warned. "Do you know what you're doing? What you're asking?"

"Isn't this what we're here to find out? If three is for me?" Her eyes moved from one to the other.

Gunnar growled low in his throat, the bright blue of his eyes even darker than they were when he kissed her earlier. "It is," he replied. "Or it's what we hoped."

"Well," she cupped each breast. "I said this place looked like something out of a storybook, but I don't know a single tale where the princess called the shots, let alone has two princes." Her thumbs grazed wet nipples. "Why don't we take it one chapter at a time? See if we fit."

TWELVE

The way she stressed the word was all the invitation Damen needed. He scooped her into his arms and turned on his heel toward the bedroom. Gunner followed, his eyes on Henley as the omega dumped her onto the coverlet.

She grinned at his playful toss, rolling onto her back and scooting up to lay back against the pile of pillows at the center. "Room for everyone," she smirked, patting the bed on each side of her. "Like the sitcom said, '*Three's Company.*'"

"Sitcom?" Gunnar asked, raising an eyebrow.

"Don't ask," Damen replied shrugging out of his shirt and dropping it to the floor.

Gunnar did the same with a smirk on his lips. "Unless it's a new sexual position, I don't need to know."

Golden hair dusted Gunnar's chest, cresting down in a gilt V along his muscled torso. Henley licked her lips as the guys each took a side and crawled onto the bed. She reached for the buttons on each of their pants. One by one, she undid each button, slowly revealing gorgeous muscles and their dark and light nether regions, respectively.

Gunnar took her hand from his fly and lifted her wrist to kiss the tender under flesh, as Damen knelt by her head. He bent, taking her mouth with his, drawing her lower lip through his teeth while Gunnar cupped her pussy, stroking the seam of her smooth lips.

The feel of them both sent heat racing across her skin and she closed her eyes.

This was beyond belief.

Mouthwatering, sexy-yummy beyond belief!

Back home this would never happen. Never. Not to girls like her and not with guys like them. Threesomes broke all the rules, but right now rules were for cowards and her inner adventure junkie was squealing *yayaah*! Both men and their amazing bodies were hers for the moment, and maybe more. Close enough to touch and taste.

Henley knew what they wanted. In their own way, they had made it clear she was the one. Their mate. *Theirs.* As in completed their triad.

The magnitude of what they wanted hit her in that moment and she stiffened.

"Henley?" Damen questioned, slipping his fingers under her chin so she looked at him. "What is it, love? Don't you want us?"

"I...I—"

"Henley," Gunnar tried. "There's no pressure, sweetheart. It's okay. Neither of us would even make you do anything you didn't want."

Damen helped her sit up, and then cupped her chin. "You know how I feel about you, baby. Since the moment we met. It's no secret. I've waited to have you, love." He let go of her chin and lifted both hands. "My hands are no longer tied. Gunnar's here and that opens a whole new world for all of us."

"I've said you're *fire*," Gunnar began. "But I didn't mean just your temper. I meant you've sparked the fire that woke my inner bear, Damen's inner bear. It's you, love. You."

Henley looked between then. "I don't know what to say to that. I thought we could just play and then I'd see, but the last thing I want is to lead you on and then not be what you imagined."

The words were so alien in her ears she almost laughed. Girls like her weren't the ones who *did* the misleading, they were the ones mislead.

"Is that what you're afraid of? That once we get a glimpse of the real you that we won't want you?" Damen replied, doubtful. "You forget that I've known you for almost a year and I've seen you in the morning with raccoon eyes and bedhead. I've been on the receiving end of your foul temper and your amazing kindness. In time, Gunnar will as well. You are everything we've ever imagined Henley."

Gunnar nodded. "And if there was any doubt at all, our bears would know." He grinned, leaning down to kiss her throat at the base of her ear. "Plus, we've already seen you naked. Very *Tata-liscious.*"

"Dude, where the hell did you get that word?" Damen turned, incredulous.

Gunnar shrugged. "I looked it up. We're courting an Earth girl, right? I wanted the lingo."

Henley looked at them both and then burst out laughing. "Okay, now that alone is reason enough to give this threesome a chance."

With a smirk, she leaned back on the pillows and planted her feet on the mattress, letting her knees fall open. She snaked her hand down her belly to her smooth mound, and then looked at them each. "Now, where were we?" She waited for their mutually stunned expressions to fade to absolute desire, as she toyed with her pussy.

The two remained silent, licking their lips.

"Are you saying what I think you're saying?" Damen asked.

Moving her free hand to the back of his neck, she nodded. "Ready for a little playtime?"

In seconds, Gunnar slipped between her legs, running his hands over her thick thighs. He pushed his pants over his hips, freeing his cock. Damen stripped, leaving a trail of clothes as he tossed them backward off the bed.

Naked, Damen's mouth took hers as his hands slid from her shoulders to her tits. Gunnar flicked her clit with the tip of his tongue before slipping the rest of the way out of his pants and boots. Hooking one hand under her thighs, he kissed her inner flesh, his free hand roaming the full curve of her ass and between her legs.

Henley moaned into Damen's kiss, his fingers working her breasts, kneading the plump mounds, his thumbs grazing her nipples until they stiffened to hard peaks. He broke their kiss, trailing his tongue over her throat to her collarbone and below, dipping his mouth to the tight, puckered bud.

She wrapped her hand around Damen's thick shaft and rolled her thumb over his wide head, her long fingers running his corded length.

She worked Damen as Gunnar pushed her knees wide to accommodate his shoulders and chest as he buried his face in her soft wet folds.

"Your pussy is so slick and swollen, love. My cock is ready to burst just looking at you." He lifted his head from between her legs, using his fingers to spread her pretty pink pussy lips apart.

"*Mmmm,*" he moaned tonguing her clit. "Juicy and sweet."

Gunnar slipped two fingers through her slick slit, curling them up to her spot, rotating his tips as he sucked her hard nub. Pulsed movements, round and round, slow then fast, then slow, had Henley arching her back as he stroked her clit with the flat of his tongue.

She ground her pussy farther into his mouth and hand until her head fell back and she cried out, spasms taking her lower body as she came.

Damen claimed her mouth again. "Straddle my cock, babe," he whispered against her lips. "I want your wet pussy circling my dick, milking my hard length with every roll of your hips."

He kissed her deeply, his tongue wrestling with hers as Gunnar helped her up. Damen released her mouth only long enough for her to hover over his bulging head before plunging herself down, taking him deep with one stroke.

He hissed, his fingers gripping her waist as

she rode him, hips rolling as his cock thrust deep into her snug slit.

Gunnar ran a hand over her back to her ass, cupping the fleshy globe. He reached around to her clit and worked her outside while Damen worked her inside. Fingers slick with her juice, he slipped around again, circling her tight hole while his other hand gripped her breasts. He ringed the rim of her ass, teasing her slickness inward before sliding one finger slowly inside.

She groaned at the shameless feel of his invasion. He released her and she arched, lifting her hips again but then sucked in a breath, tensing at the feel of Gunnar's thick head against her tight ring instead of his fingers.

"Relax, baby. Close your eyes and let me in," Gunnar whispered. "Let me fill you, deep from behind as Damen stuffs you good from the front."

Adrenaline coursed through her veins and Gunnar growled at the scent. He reached around again, cupping her pussy. Damen sucked her tits while Gunnar kept his cock prone and ready. He circled her clit, rubbing and working her until her head dropped back onto Gunnar's shoulder and she cried out, coming hard.

One hand splayed on her belly, Gunnar tensed, waiting. Damen pulled Henley forward, his mouth finding hers, and the act lifted her ass prone. Gunnar spread her cheeks, and pressed his head through her snug entrance. She froze at the alien feel, but Damen kissed her deeper, demanding and hungry.

Her breath locked in her throat at the feel of Gunnar taking her inch by inch until his cock stretched her body and the only thing separating the two men was a thin layer of her flesh. Her body pulsed with forbidden pleasure, her legs weak as Gunnar and Damen filled her.

A final orgasm ripped through her, sending her mind whirling. Both men growled at her cry, feral and full of need, the power of her spasms sending them over the edge as they emptied themselves deeply within her.

They held tightly, letting aftershocks take them until Henley slumped onto Damen's chest and Gunnar covered her back, spent and sweaty.

"Hen—" Damen shifted his head, craning to look at her. "You alive?"

She smiled against his sweat-sheened skin. "I don't know. Do dead people have throbby bits?"

He grinned. "I don't think so."

"Then I'm as alive as I'll ever be. Just don't ask me to move. I haven't recovered enough brain power to think how."

Gunnar moved her damp hair from her shoulders and feathered kisses along the back of her neck and shoulder. "So, what do you think?"

She inhaled, looking at him from the corner of her eye. "Let me get back to you on that. I've got system overload there too."

He straightened from her, letting his still stiff member slide from her slowly before helping her off Damen's lap. The three lay in a cuddled heap in the dim moonlight.

"We stink," she chuckled. "And I'm as stiff as your cocks. Maybe we should try that inside hot spring in there." She let a weak hand drift toward the bathroom.

Gunner kissed the top of one breast, letting his tongue circle her nipple. "We could. Or you could let us take you to a real hot spring tomorrow. Show you what mountain life can offer. Summit isn't the sleepy isolated clan it used to be. That's what I tried to tell Damen in my emails."

"Oh for the love of —" he broke off. "I told you, I never got your communiques. Do you really think I wouldn't have come home had you told me everything you said earlier?"

Gunnar lifted his face from Henley's breast, and shrugged. "I sent one a week."

"Who sent them? You personally?" Damen asked.

Henley sat up at that.

"Well?"

Gunnar shook his head. "No. I gave them to Naz Voda. Our liaison to the Lord Chamberlain in the Palladian palace."

"Ding. Ding. Ding," Henley said sitting up between them. "There's your answer right there. Maddox betrayed Vander and the house of Kasaval and your guy betrayed you. He must have known if Damen came back, he'd sniff out their black market bingo and bring Vander and every warrior available to squash their plans. They had to keep Damen away to ensure Vander and everyone else was kept in the dark."

Damen's jaw tightened as his eyes found Gunnar's. "Where is Naz Voda now?"

Gunnar looked between the two as they waited. "No one has seen him for at least ten months. We assumed he was killed in an avalanche. His pack and one boot were found at the base of the middle ridge."

"The same amount of time since Maddox was poisoned and Jag killed Bors and Sharan Dul. It all fits," Henley said.

Damen nodded. "If your guy is dead, maybe it's because he was headed to warn the Hatun." He thought for a moment. "We'd better let Vander know so he can send reinforcements. I don't want to leave Henley here without trained warriors to protect her and the Summit. If the Hatun know we're coming, then the northern slope mountain rogues do as well."

"Wait a minute," Henley looked between the two of them. "Who said anything about leaving Henley behind like the little woman? I've very capable, and you know it." She glared at Damen. "I've been a strategic asset since I arrived from Earth, you've said so a billion times. Or was that just sweet talk to get in my pants?"

Gunnar groaned. "This is so not the pillow talk I was hoping for. C'mon you two. We just had amazing sex and got this threesome off the ground. What is the Earth phrase? We have lift off? Let's table this for now and spend the next couple of days getting to know each other...inside and out and everywhere in between." He said gliding his hand up Henley's thigh.

She pushed his hand aside. "That might work with some other girl, Gunnar. But this girl is a fighter. I want in on this and if you two want in on *this* again," her hand went to her nether regions, "then we need to talk. I can't consider being part of a threesome or forever triad if I'm simply your *little woman.*"

"Well," Damen said teasing. "You are pretty small."

She rolled her eyes. "Yeah, said no one on

Earth, ever. Maybe compared to you two tree trunks, but that's not what I mean and you know it."

"I do, but if something happened to you I'd never…we'd never forgive ourselves," he replied.

Gunnar nodded. "Damen's right. We can't risk it."

"Well then. I stowed away once, I can stow away again. And if there's no place for me to sneak into, then I'll track you. I can do that you know. I was a private investigator back on earth. I have skills." She sniffed. "It's your choice. Either I go with you with your full knowledge so you can do whatever protective possessive thing you shifters do, or I come on the sneak."

Gunnar slipped his fingers up her thighs to her belly. "Looks like our girl likes to do things the hard way."

Damen chuckled cupping her breast. "Okay, Hen. You win. But in exchange we get to show you how we play hard, over and over again."

She sighed as his mouth took her nipple while Gunnar's hand slid to her still throbbing sex. "If you must," she murmured.

THIRTEEN

Henley woke alone. Bright sun streamed in from the large windows and she blinked. For a girl who got almost no sleep, she felt amazing. Energy coursed through her body despite her sore bits. Well used. She giggled to herself at the words. Every woman in the universe should wake up once in her life feeling that satisfied.

Rolling over, she squished both pillows on either side of her head to her face and inhaled. Damen and Gunnar. God, their combined scent could make her come. Especially with the naughty images running through her head, and for once in her life, they weren't fantasies.

She bounded out of bed and headed for the bathroom. Her stomach growled demandingly, warring with the need to find the guys and pinch herself that this was really real.

Turning on the shower spray, the water warmed immediately. Rose scented and the perfect temperature. She rummaged through the bathroom closet for toiletries and a towel and then stepped into the spray. Warm jets eased sore muscles and she soaped up a soft cloth to wash her more tenders bits. Wash rinse repeat was next for her long hair and she turned off the shower, stepping out onto the mat.

She dried quickly, squeezing as much water from her hair as she could before brushing the thick dark mass into her signature high ponytail. Padding naked from the bath, she grabbed her pack for her makeup but then decided against it. Gunnar said something about a hot spring, and Damen had already teased about seeing her with raccoon eyes.

Voices outside the window caught her attention, and she walked over, peeking out from behind the sheers. Damen and Gunnar were outside. Movement in her window caught Damen's attention and he shielded his eyes to look up. A softball sized snowball whizzed from behind hitting him square in the back and he whirled around.

"You're a dead man, brother bear!"

She grinned at their laughter and rushed to get dressed.

* * *

"Good morning, my lady," the same young girl from the day before greeted her with a smile. "There's plenty for breakfast in the morning room." She pointed to a large arched doorway across the expansive foyer.

The lodge itself was rustic and beautiful with high dark-beamed ceilings and stonework. The main staircase was wide and curved with a thick carpet runner in the center in a deep crimson.

Henley stepped off the bottom stair and gave the girl a soft smile before heading in search of food. Her stomach growled again, and delicious aromas coming through the doorway had her picking up her pace.

She stopped inside the breakfast room door and took in the floor to ceiling windows that over looked an impressive vista. This part of the chalet was built on the edge of the ridge, so the windows made it seem as though you hung off the edge of a cliff.

A long polished table sat at the center of the room, and behind it was an extra-long sideboard piled with food. Hot chafing dishing steamed with eggs and meats while deep tureens bubbled with porridge thick with sausage and cream.

Henley grabbed a plate and walked the impressive choices before filling her dish. She sat at one end of the table alone, taking pains to eat slowly despite being starved.

Damen walked in and she looked up from her breakfast and smiled, pressing her lips together at the heat flushing her cheeks at the teasing look on his face.

"Don't look at me like that or everyone will know what we did last night," she whispered as he took a seat beside her.

He lifted her hand and kissed it, letting his smirk spread across her knuckles. "Everyone already does. Get used to it. Part of being royalty in a small clan. Can't poop without everyone knowing what color it was."

"Ugh, Damen. I'm trying to eat." She made a face, but couldn't help the grin tugging at her lips.

He kissed her quickly and then got up from the table. "Eat up. We've got to get moving."

"Why? Where are we going?"

He lifted one finger and then rushed out, coming back almost as fast carrying a pair of fur and oiled skin boots, a fur lined coat and what looked to be snowshoes. He put them on a chair and nodded. "For you," he said. "A gift from me and Gunnar to our girl."

She laughed, wiping her mouth. "Am I joining the Olympics or is this some kind of mountain man test to see if I can stand roughing it?"

"Where we're headed isn't an easy trek, but so worth the effort. We're taking you springing," he said.

Breaking off a piece of soft sweet bread peppered with dried fruit and citrus, she chewed looking at him. "I hope that's not some sort of shifter style ski jump thing, because it sounds sweaty, and I'm not dressed for sweaty."

"It's not, and you look beautiful. This is a surprise, so finish eating. Gunnar is waiting for us in the stables."

"The stables?" she questioned.

He nodded. "He's getting our mounts packed."

"Mounts? As in horses?"

Damen grinned. "Not exactly. You'll see."

Henley sat back surprised as he motioned for her to follow, taking the snowshoe thingies with him. She finished the last of her juice and wiped her mouth before pushing back from the table. Smoothing the crimson tunic trimmed with black fur, she glanced at her reflection is the mirrored wall behind the food. The color was perfect for her, and the outfit was comfortable and flattering. She smiled to herself, confidence brimming.

She grabbed the coat and boots, and hurried

after Damen. They walked through the expansive lobby and down a flight of stairs toward the back. The air chilled as they descended until she shivered, slipping the coat over her shoulders.

"Does it ever warm up around here?" she asked.

He nodded. "In summer. When the sands boil around the capital and it's too hot to move, the weather at the Summit is gorgeous. It doesn't last long, maybe a month and a half. Two if we're lucky."

"Great," she grumbled. "Cold and wet, all day, all the time."

He laughed as they reached the bottom landing. "It's not that bad, Hen. There's bright sunshine most days. That is when it's not storming. Think of all the fun we can have in front of the fire."

"Naked on a bearskin rug?" she raised an eyebrow.

He rolled his eyes. "God no! But naked on a *bear*, definitely!" Damen winked and moved to open a heavy door. He pushed it wide and motioned for Henley to go first.

She walked through and then stopped. "Holy shit! Are those llamas?"

Gunnar looked up from strapping on the last saddle. "Alpacas, actually." He fastened the last buckle and then was in front of her with two long strides. "Good morning," he said, leaning in to brush his lips over hers. "Sleep well?"

She shoved his shoulder back and the pushed past him to stare at the funny long-necked beasts. "We're riding on llamas. You do realize these things spit, right? Or at least they do in the Earth version."

Gunnar moved past her to pick up the reins on the first beast. "Same animal, actually. I had a few dozen brought in from Earth on a transport once we modernized. They were Naz Voda's idea." He frowned for a moment.

"Probably got them when Maddox had the latest Arabian steeds brought in for us from Earth," Damen added. "The two of them. Naz Voda and Maddox. Fucking pair of treasonous snakes."

Henley shook her head. "It's a bitch, but I trust you two, Vander and Jag will dole out whatever's necessary once you get to the bottom of it." She looked around the stables. "Speaking of Jag, where is he? I haven't seen him since I watched him race off with two wolves last evening."

"He's not back yet. Being a prince of the realm, it's not often Jag gets a chance to race the moons just for the hell of it. He won't be back until Vander sends the transport to take us to the southern steppes on the outskirts of the Tempera jungle."

She looked at them both. "We're really not going to hike?"

Gunnar and Damen exchanged a look, and then Gunnar shook his head. "It's too dangerous with the northern rogues. Since you insisted on coming, we need to minimize the risks."

"He's right," Damen nodded. "Even if the Hatun don't know we're coming, the rogues are always looking for ways to make easy money. You're a royal envoy and tantamount to being part of the royal family, not to mention possibly our mate." He winked. "Hint, hint."

"That's right, so no hiking or exploring on your own. This means no taking matters into your own hands, however capable," Gunnar continued. "The Kasaval have an edge since their xenos transforms into an immense ancient lion. We're polar bears. Not the same kind of fire power in the jungle as on the mountain."

She cocked her head. "Where I come from, there are only a handful of animals listed as man-eaters, ones who will hunt and attack humans even when not provoked. Polar bears are on that list." She smirked. "Looking at you two, my guess is you're as deadly as the Kasaval lion regardless of the climate."

Damen moved behind her and slipped his arms around her waist. "When it comes to protecting you? Deadly doesn't even begin to cover it."

"Okay, enough doom and gloom. Today is all about showing you the perks of mountain life," Gunnar said, patting the Alpaca's saddle. "Mount up. We're burning daylight."

FOURTEEN

"These llamas are surprisingly even keeled," Henley said, squirming in her saddle. "I wish I could say the same for my butt."

Damen laughed. "I don't think your ass is sore from the saddle, love. I think that honor goes to Gunnar."

"Hey, could have been you just as easily, dude. In fact, it will be next time, so shut up. Henley's ass is magic," Gunner huffed.

Henley burst out laughing. "I appreciate the compliment, but my magic ass is having a hard time right now, so stop." She looked at the craggy, snow covered path and winced. "Talk about something else. Take my mind off the bump and grind killing my backside."

"Girl, if it's a bump and grind you want, we can certainly deliver a kind that will definitely take your mind off things," Damen joked.

"Damen, no. Tell me more about this Naz Voda. Do you really think he was in cahoots with Maddox? Sharan Dul was behind Maddox's poisoning, so maybe it was his cronies that took out your guy."

Gunnar shrugged. "This morning I sent men to look for evidence on where Naz was headed. I want to know for sure if he's dead."

"True." Damen nodded. "We made the mistake of assuming Bors was dead after he abducted Ivy, but he wasn't and got to Riley next. Jag took him out, though. Ripped the poor bastard to shreds."

Henley wiggled in her saddle. "Hey, you long-necked fur ball. Quit it!"

"What?" Gunnar asked, urging his mount closer.

She swiped at the animal's flank. "This snow beast keeps chewing on my boot and it tickles, not to mention it keeps untying the laces." She unclasped her foot from the stirrup, and reached for the crisscrossed ties. "Stupid spitball factory!"

With Henley partially bent, tying her boot, the alpaca charged. Running at top speed with Henley bouncing in her saddle, she held on for dear life. She wrapped her arms around the beast's neck, and screamed for Damen.

Gunnar raced up the trail, each reaching for the runaway reins. He gripped the bolting llama's harness and pulled it to a stop. Damen slowed as well, jumping off his mount to let Henley slid from hers to his arms.

"You okay?" he asked, chuckling as he cradled her against his chest.

"It's not funny. That phlegm ball could've killed me," she sniffed.

Grinning, Gunnar held both sets of reins in his big hand. "Don't blame the beast, love. You took your foot out of the stirrup and that signaled him to run."

"Still, I'm riding with one of you on the way back. That camel wannabe can fall off a cliff for all I care." She sniffed again.

Gunnar laughed. "Lucky for us, our surprise is on the other side of that short rise." He took the reins from Damen and tied the three alpacas to a tree on the side of the trail.

The three walked the rest of the way up the slope. At the dip at the top, there was a small opening in the rock face. Henley looked at the two guys, angling her head. "Is that it? That's the surprise?"

"Nope," Gunnar replied. "Your surprise is on the other side."

He went first, holding his hand out for

Henley to help her up into the narrow entrance. Water dripped on the rock walls inside, and the narrow passage opened after about ten feet to a large cavern. The walls were damp and moss covered, and gorgeous purple and yellow flowers grew in clusters from cracks in the rock. It was like springtime inside, and she grinned.

"This is gorgeous," she said, looking around. "How, though? It's ice cold outside. Is the mountain volcanic?"

Damen shook his head. "Not exactly, but there is a natural heat source that gives off just enough warmth and humidity for this to blossom year round." He smiled. "Want to see?"

She took his hand and he led her down a carved path that wound in a wide spiral with wildflowers and succulents growing out of crevices along the edges. At the base, the path ended at a natural crater that looked almost volcanic in nature and inside was water that shimmered pink with steamy smoke curling from the surface.

Gunnar came up beside them and slipped an arm around Henley's waist. "Surprise," he murmured.

"This is the hot spring we told you about last night. Pretty cool, huh." Damen nodded.

"You know what's even better?" Stripping

out of his clothes, Gunnar left them in a pile on the side where a carved bench was hewn into the rock and then dove into the pink depths. He came up, flipping his blond hair to the side. "This!"

Damen did the same, cannonballing into the water so he splashed Henley, soaking her clothes.

She sputtered, jumping back. "Not cool, Damen! I'm dripping!"

He swam to the edge of the spring and grinned. "That's the whole idea, love. We want you dripping and wet and sexy as hell, so lay your clothes on the bench and get your sweet ass in here with us."

"I'm going to freeze on the way back," she mumbled, and he laughed splashing her again.

After undressing, Henley turned, and staring him down, walked to the edge and did a backflip straight into the water. She surfaced with a grin. "Eighth grade swim team. Boys and Girls Club of America."

He laughed, swimming toward her to scoop her up in his arms. She circled her legs around his waist, leaning back so her full breasts bobbed in the water as her dark hair floated around her like a dark cloud.

Gunnar swam to them and lifted her shoulders to rest on his chest, his hands cupping her breasts in the water. "C'mon, luscious.

There's a built-in bench along the edge." Gunnar let go and she unwrapped her legs from Damen, and the three swam together to the side.

Both met her eyes with a hungry gaze. The carved bench was wide, much wider than she expected when Damen lifted her to it easily. "You don't know how the thought of you occupies my brain, Henley. I've never wanted anyone like this. I want to more than fuck you, beautiful." He kissed her lips, a tender, soft heart clenching kiss.

Gunnar moved to flank her opposite thigh and he leaned in to nip her ear, letting his tongue trace the soft tender flesh. "I've had your ass, and now I want your hot wet pussy so fucking bad, I can't see straight."

She couldn't breathe for the want of both men. Gunnar and Damen pulled her back into the water, and Damen hopped up to the bench. He moved his knees apart, just enough for Henley to slip between them. The water barely covered the stone, and his erect cock jutted straight up as he leaned back on the soft moss.

For all her fire, she was putty in their hands, and she didn't argue when Damen fisted her hair. "You have the sexiest mouth, love. I want to watch my dick disappear between your luscious lips." He gently pushed her face toward his cock.

She smirked, sparing a glance for him as her tongue darted forward to lick his swollen head.

His dark eyes flashed with red and he groaned, his lids closing for a moment. Gunner moved in behind her, his hands on her waist as she bent to taste more of Damen.

"Take his cock in your hot little cunt, Henley. Let me watch you as Gunnar fucks you, then take my dick deep as I fuck your mouth."

Henley lowered her head and took Damen's cock deep and then released him with a pop. Glancing over her shoulder, she licked her lips as Gunnar teased her soft folds. Her slick pussy slippery on his fingers in the pink water. "Easy access, babe," she said, arching her back for him. "Dealer's choice. Ass or slit."

He slipped his thumb into her wet cleft and used his fingers to tease her clit. He circled the hard nub with his middle finger, cupping her entire sex in his palm. She arched more and lifted her head, letting the ends of her hair float in the water.

With no warning, Gunnar grabbed her hips, driving his cock deep with one thrust. "I love the way the water drips off of you. Makes me want to lick your skin from your cunt to your mouth."

Her body exploded at his raw words. Her cunt squeezing his cock as she came hard. Her mouth went slack as every muscle in her body tensed, riding the wave. Damen bent to nibble her lips, and her mouth took his, her lips parting so he could fuck her mouth with his tongue as aftershocks spasmed through her core.

He broke their kiss and with her mouth still open, whispered, "Suck me, babe. Take every drop. Let my hot cum run down your throat."

She gasped, plunging her mouth onto his waiting dick, flattening her tongue to suck him deep. Teasing, she milked his corded length as Gunnar thrust and held over and over, reaching around to tease her clit as his cock filled her from behind.

Tension built and she whimpered as a final climax took her. She let go, ripping her mouth from Damen's dick as she cried out. Guttural and raw, Gunner roared emptying himself deep within her.

Henley tensed, her body clenching around his cock. She wrapped a hand around Damen's hard length and ran her fingers over his head before taking him into her throat again. She sucked, working his corded mass until he dug his fingers into her hair tighter, his head swelling in her mouth.

With a growl he came hard. Hot jets squirting into her mouth and down her throat. She let the salty cream run over her hand as she squeezed every drop from him. He slumped back, letting his hands slip from the tangle of her hair to her face as he lifted her from his still hard member.

"You are one talented girl," he chuckled.

Gunnar kissed the middle of her back and slid from her as well. He let his fingers trailed over her shoulder as he moved around to her side, helping her straighten. "One of these times, I'm going to get to watch your face as you come."

She wiped her mouth and then smiled. "Maybe you'll get to watch my face as you mark me. I hear it's a trippy experience."

Both men stared at her. "Are you saying what I think you're saying?" Damen asked. "You want to stay with us?"

She shrugged. "I'm thinking about it. Seriously. To be honest, it's all I've been thinking about since last night."

Gunner pulled her into his arms, slipping his fingers under her chin so she looked him in the eye. "You realize what marking you means, right? It means we've claimed you as ours. Our mate. Completing our triad."

"I know." She nodded. "It's a big step, and that's why I said I'm thinking about it. Ivy and Riley are my best friends. They're sisters-in-law now. I'm not sure I want to be so far away from them." She looked at Damen. "You've been with Vander and Jag for fifteen years, you must know what I mean…my reservations."

He nodded. "I do. But the Summit is my home. All the problems I had before ended when Gunnar defied Cero. The old bear is toothless now. Literally and figuratively. So there's nothing stopping me from being here and fulfilling my destiny. Nothing stopping me, but you."

She took his words and they made her heart clench. "I think you know I've been in love with you for ages, Damen."

He nodded again, and leaned to kiss the side of her hair. "I know."

"But my feelings for you have changed over these past few days." Her eyes found Gunnar and she looked between them. "Torn between two lovers," she sang with a shrug, chuckling. "It's a corny Earth song."

Gunnar turned her chin again. "Except you know you don't have to choose between us."

"A package deal with two guys with quite the packages."

She chewed on her lip. "I'll let you know my decision once we get back from this expedition." She shrugged again. "I hope that's okay."

Gunnar circled her waist from the front, and Damen jumped down, doing the same from behind. "Of course, love."

FIFTEEN

A hot billowing wind churned over the landing site as the hover transport descended to its coordinated mark. Engines roared once more and then cut as the transport shut down, its lights going dark.

A metal bridge plank lowered from the side and Vander ducked beneath the exit portal to walk down to greet his brother and the others waiting. The king was flanked by a small squad of warriors.

"An entourage, bro?" Jag chuckled, greeted his brother with a hug. "You didn't need to make the trip yourself, let alone with a contingent."

"The contingent isn't for you. It's in case Henley has to go kicking and screaming. Ivy's having a fit she left without a word."

Damen snorted at that. "Left? Tried stowed

away." He laughed, pulling Vander into a hug. He turned then and gestured to Gunnar. "Vander, this is Gunnar Lukas, alpha of the Summit Clan."

Gunnar held his hand out and Vander took it. "You're welcome here, Your Majesty."

"Please, it's Vander. With Damen between us, we're practically family. Especially since my brother informs me you and Damen have found your mate and completed your triad."

Exchanging a quick look with Damen, he nodded. "Yes, but not if you're planning to take her back to the capital." He smirked. "Kicking and screaming, to use your words. She still needs a bit of convincing."

Vander laughed. "Comes with the territory when your mate is human. They're difficult, but worth the effort, trust me. Unfortunately, Henley is one of three and they're all as much fire as they are trouble. My queen included. She's beside herself, and since she just gave birth to my son, I can't have her upset."

"Tell Ivy to relax and stop worrying, V," Henley said, walking toward the men as they stood on the landing pad. "I'm fine."

Vander looked at the tall, statuesque woman as she approached. "For all the trouble you've caused me, I should drag you back, so Ivy can give you the face full you deserve, instead of me. She's been worried sick. Her and Riley both."

"I'm sorry, V. I didn't plan on stowing away. Damen and I…I…talked the night before he left, and I couldn't leave it that way. I had to know." She paused, raising her chin as she looked at the king. "You would have done the same if it was Ivy leaving."

Vander considered her for a moment. "You're right. I would have. Without a second thought for anyone. Do me a favor, though. The Summit has top communication technology now. Call Ivy. Do it in a hologram so she can see what I see."

"Oh," she smirked. "And what is it you think you see?"

The king's face softened, and he smiled at his mate's best friend. "That you're happy and that you've decided to stay because you've found your mates."

"Well," Henley smirked, ignoring the heat in her cheeks at what was implied in Vander's polite words. "The jury's still deliberating on that, but the odds look pretty good."

The king nodded. "Well, then, that's a horse of a different color even if I say so myself."

"Ivy got you watching Earth movies again?" Henley laughed.

He smirked. "Wizard of Oz. She said it's a classic for the kids."

"Yeah, well, those flying monkeys scared the shit out of me as a kid, so I don't know about that."

Vander held out his arms and she grinned, walking into his hug. The king kissed the top of her head and gave her a squeeze. "Call Ivy. If not for her sake, then for mine."

She chuckled. "I will. I promise." Stepping back, she looked up at him. "Funny Gerri wasn't able to calm her down."

"Yeah, well. Gerri is busy on Earth right now. Family of one of her matches is making trouble."

Henley laughed out loud. "You mean like Riley and I did about Alvia and your mate did about Cassie?" She shook her head. "Poor Gerri. If anyone can handle meddlesome friends and family, it's her and whoever it is might end up with a match of their own. Just look at us."

"I hate to break up this reunion, but we've got a job to do, remember? That was the whole point of coming here in the first place." Jag interrupted. "Everything's ready to load into the hovercraft."

Vander nodded. "Let my men do that. I'm starving. Plus, I want a quick tour of the Summit and a fast brief on your plan to date and anything else you've found."

* * *

Jag walked down the transport plank from the main cabin. "Looks like we're all set. Everybody ready?"

Gunnar nodded, picking up the last of their packs. Vander gestured to Damen, calling him to the side. "I'm not happy about Henley going with you," the king said, shaking his head. "I could forbid it, but I won't. I may live to regret it sooner than later, like the moment Ivy finds out, but I trust you. Plus, I don't like the idea of not carrying fusion weapons. I know this is an expedition, but the whole idea is to destroy the lot of them if you find the Unduru."

"I know, Vander, but Henley didn't give us much choice. She stowed away once already, and knowing her stubbornness, she'd probably follow regardless of what we said. It was better to say yes and keep her close, you know?" Damen replied. "As for weapons, I got us covered fusion wise." He patted his waist and his pack.

The king gave his friend a perceptive smile. "Good. I knew I could count on you to speak softly but carry a fusion powered laser." He grinned. "As for Henley…she's cut from the same cloth as the others. All of them. As difficult as they are beautiful."

He exhaled before continuing. "If you can avoid catastrophe, this could prove your triad bond truly unbreakable, BUT I don't have to remind you what's at stake if something happens to Henley. Not just for you and Gunnar, but for me as well."

Damen nodded. "Don't I know it, bro. Gunnar and I would sacrifice ourselves before anything happened to our mate." He clapped his friend on the shoulder. "That you can count on."

The two headed up the gangplank, Damen's eyes catching Henley's in one of the transport windows. They were heading into the unknown, and suddenly their compromise with Henley seemed reckless and unthinking. If it wasn't so serious, he'd laugh.

He accused her of being just that. Reckless and unthinking. He exhaled again. At least it was a calculated decision, and not one made with their dicks. Then again, if they lost her — he shook his head. Failure was not an option.

The transport hatch closed and locked and the hovercraft rose from the launch pad and maneuvered up and over the summit's highest point before steering toward their drop point. Reaching the lower northern slopes this way saved them days of hiking in less than friendly territory.

Damen looked out the window at the rugged terrain and Henley leaned over his shoulder to see. "The slopes are so steep. Are they as impassable as they look, or do they just seem that way from this vantage point?" she asked.

He shook his head. "They're pretty treacherous. That's why we would've hiked down our trails to the base of the southern Mirror Mountain and then crossed the lower gorge to the northern side. It takes longer, but there's no risk of avalanche at that elevation."

"How does Vander plan to land this thing? There doesn't look like there's a flat space anywhere?" she said, craning her neck.

Damen smirked. "He's not. We're diving again."

Henley's eyes jerked from the window to his amused face. "You're not serious. How? The terrain is too rocky, plus look at those trees, we'll be impaled or break our necks or something."

"What happened, love? Your inner adventure junkie decide to bail?" He chuckled.

She bristled, but when she opened her mouth to argue, she stopped, inching closer to the transport window again. "Damen, I thought I just saw —"

He raised a questioning brow and slipped in

beside her. Movement was clear and present on the narrow trails and in the tree line. He frowned, getting up from his seat to slip in beside Gunnar and Jag.

"We have company," he said and they both turned.

Jag looked out his window, his eyes tracking where Damen pointed. "Rogues."

Vander walked in from the pilot deck. "It looks like we've been spotted."

"Now what?" Gunnar asked.

Jag exchanged a glance with Vander before his brother replied. "The transport has the royal seal, so the rogues probably don't think this has anything to do with the Summit. They probably think this is an exploratory flight. Benign."

"Exploratory. For what?" Gunnar asked.

Jag shrugged. "Does it matter? The royal seal gives us an out. The most they can try for is a kidnap and a ransom. They don't know the real reasons we're in the territory, so if we pay them off ahead of time, you know, under the pretext of guides," he paused, crooking his fingers, "then they'll have a reason to walk the line."

Damen agreed. "Their money train ended six months ago when Maddox disappeared. They might know he was poisoned. They might not. But money talks and what are the Hatun going to pay them with? Shrunken heads?"

"They might even know what happened to Naz Voda. Enough coin will definitely loosen their lips, especially if they think we're picking up where Maddox left off," Gunnar added. "If my gut is right, Maddox and Naz Voda only told the rogues enough to keep their interest. Chances are they'll keep their distance, though. Wait for an opportunity to grab and go."

Vander's eyes moved to Henley before looking back at the three men ready to roll. "What about your girl? This changes things. Maybe I should take her back to the Palladian palace with me."

"I'm sitting right here, V. It's not like I can't hear you four talking and strategizing," she said, getting up to stand in the aisle between them. "I'm not going back to the capital. Unless you drag me back by royal edict, forget it. Besides, you four have forgotten the most important carrot you've got."

"Carrot?" Gunnar asked.

She nodded. "Bait."

Her word hit home and he stood, shaking his head. "No. Absolutely not. We are not using you as bait. Not to entice the rogues and certainly not for the Hatun to lure the Unduru. No."

Damen shook his head, agreeing with his

alpha. "There are too many variables that can go wrong, Hen. We said we'd take you with us only if you promised you wouldn't do anything rash, remember?"

"I'm not planning anything, trust me. I may be reckless sometimes, but I'm not stupid. I'm not about to put myself in harm's way. Not for real, anyway. I'm talking about my presence. Jag just said the most the rogues could try is kidnap and ransom. With me along, it's bound to be something at the back of their minds if you three don't pony up or you try something fishy.

"Or they might try to double dip. Take what you offer and then take me for more. Either way, keeping me around will definitely keep their interest enough until we pass into the jungle. My guess is they won't follow." She shrugged. "Maybe Gunnar is right and they'll keep to the shadows until an opportunity presents itself. We need to make sure one doesn't."

Gunnar exchanged a look with Damen before shifting to Jag. "What do you think? Damen and I can't make this decision. We're too personally involved. Right now my inner bear is ready to tear someone a new asshole just thinking about Henley in danger. It's got to be your call."

"As long as it's not my ass you use as a chew toy, I think Henley has a point. We'll have to be diligent. She goes nowhere alone, and I mean NO

158

WHERE." He eyed her, nodding. "Hen, that means bathroom breaks are not solo affairs. You okay with that?"

She laughed. "I've live with girls my whole life, most recently Ivy and Riley. No one pees alone."

Vander nodded. "Good, then it's settled. I'll have the pilot drop you as close to the lower steppes as possible."

Damen pulled Henley down onto his lap and kissed her cheek. "Looks like you got your wish for a hike after all. Hopefully, it's not too far from the trading post."

SIXTEEN

The transport found a way to hover close enough they were able to climb from the plank to a wide flat ridge. Packs were unloaded and two of Vander's four guards joined the expedition. Henley was surrounded five to one. The boys were serious when they meant never alone. Still, to be circled by five hot shifters, two of which were hers and hers alone, not bad by a long shot. Forget the landscape, she had her own sigh-worthy scenery to look at.

They each carried a pack, but hers was at least a third of the weight as the guys'. The cold gave way to mild weather, and she peeled her jacket from her shoulders, stuffing the puffy material into her pack when they stopped for a break. She adjusted her belt and the dagger Gunnar had given her, just in case.

"You guys don't have to stop for me. I'm

fine. As long as we can eat and drink while moving, I'm good," she said, trying to keep it light despite their hovering. "Listen, I realize I'm the lone human here, but if I'm tired or need a break I will speak up. I have a mouth and I'm not afraid to use it."

Gunnar handed her a canteen of water and then pressed a kiss to her temple. "And a talented mouth at that," he whispered.

Heat flushed her cheeks as she stole a glance to the others to make sure they hadn't heard before circling his neck with her hand. She pulled him close and quickly pressed her lips to his. "Play your cards right and you might get a shot at that mouth later."

His lips spread against her and he growled. "Baby, that's a date."

Damen caught sight and winked. "Whatever it is you two are cooking up, count me in. I can feel the heat from here."

They wound down the narrow trails, single file, with weapons ready for attacks from the trees and from the crags above. After Riley's attack six months earlier, Jag briefed them on the rogues preferred methods.

Henley kept close to Gunnar, and Damen followed behind, never more than an arm's distance from her back. A light rain fell as they reached the base. They rounded the end of the trail only to face a coursing river separating the Mirror Mountains from the edge of the Tempera. The trading post was on the opposite side and the only thing connecting them was a broken-down bridge over the wild depths."

"You've got to be kidding," she mumbled.

Gunnar glanced over his shoulder. "You game, babe?"

"Yah," she said with an exhale. "Just call me playah."

They crossed as quickly as possible, each stepping where the other had first. The last of them stepped onto the far cliff as rogues filed out from the trees on the opposite side.

"We've got company for real," Jag said, moving into fight position with the others. Damen pushed Henley behind him.

"If we have to shift, you run. Take the silver pack. It's got enough to keep you until we can find you. I'll be right behind you as soon as I can" His voice was low, but enough worry laced his tone that she nodded instead of arguing.

Lifting what looked like a machete, one of the rogues cut the bridge's anchor ropes and the entire thing splintered, crashing against the rocky gorge.

Gunnar kept his eyes on the rogues, but his

shoulders relaxed a notch. "That makes their message clear. We'll have to find another way across at the end of the week."

"Didn't you bring a transmitter thingy? With all your technology, no one's thought to make a handheld communicator? Even Star Trek has those," Henley questioned with a soft huff.

"You mean like this?" Jag lifted what looked like a small Bluetooth earpiece from his pocket. "We've got it covered, Hen. We might have to cross the river farther down because the hover transport won't be able to land or even get close with all this tree cover, but we can definitely call ahead."

She looked between Damen and Gunnar. "Do you have those as well?"

"Of course," Gunnar replied.

Switching her glare to Damen, she put her hands on her hips. "Take the silver pack, Henley. Hide. Make your home in the trees like a monkey and I'll find you," she mimicked.

"Hen—"

She snorted. "I can work a communicator, Damen. You could've handed me yours to call Vander. He's probably close enough, he could've turned around."

"Yeah, but then I wouldn't get to play hide the banana with you in the vines," he teased, kissing her nose.

Jag chuckled, but then thumbed toward the trading post. "Funny, but our journey starts there, so let's go."

The ground around the trading post was tamped down. It was clear where the terrain had been cut back, but in the year since Maddox and his black market business had been taken down, the jungle had reclaimed much of the landscape.

She walked around the front, dodging scrub and insects with wingspans like birds. "It doesn't look like anyone's been here in a while."

"Nope. Not what I was hoping." Gunnar shook his head. "I had hoped we'd find a lead or something that would help us track the Hatun other than my and Damen's combined memory."

Jag squatted by the edge of the post near the back end. "Take a look at this."

The three moved to where he bent, leaving Vander's two guards to cover. "It looks like a footprint," Gunnar said, peering closer. "Juvenile. Could be a primate or even one of the Hatun youth."

"You have those here, too?" Henley asked.

"That's a dumb question. You know we have children on Galaxa," Gunnar teased.

She rolled her eyes. "No, bear for brains.

Primates. We have a ton of varieties on Earth. From very, very small to even as big as you, though monkeys are better comedians than you."

"No doubt," Gunner joked back. "But can your primates talk?"

Henley blinked, not knowing if he was serious or just teasing again. "Talk. As in being dual-natured, talk?"

"No, as in opening their primate mouths and speaking," he replied.

Her mouth dropped and she looked from the footprint to Gunnar and then Damen, and he nodded. "It's true. Rare, but true. Some single-natured animals have developed the ability to communicate. Not in full, cognitive sentences, but in basic words and sounds. They aren't fully expressive, but they understand everything," Damen said.

Jag straightened from his squat and wiped his hands on his thighs. "Look around for anything else that might tell us who was here last. They might lead us right where we need to go."

"Do you really think the Hatun will attack? Don't they want help freeing themselves from the Unduru?" Henley asked. "I mean, who would want to live having to sacrifice their own just so they're left alone? It's like King Kong meets Dracula. If it wasn't so appalling, it'd be funny."

Damen angled his head. "King Kong? Wasn't he a giant ape or something? How does that fit this scenario?"

"Because, the natives sacrificed their women once a month to appease Kong, otherwise he'd go ape-shit on them." She lifted a hand. "The Hatun sacrifice women in kind of the same way. It's been a year since you, Vander, and Jag took down the black market Maddox made. It only follows the Hatun would have to find alternative sources or sacrifice their own. So, if that's the case and they have to sacrifice their own, why wouldn't they want our help?"

"Hey! Over here," Jag called from the opposite side of the trading post.

They rushed to where he'd brushed away a line of newly fallen leaves. Underneath were the same sort of tracks, but these weren't dried out.

"Fresh," he said pointing to the indentations in the soft ground. And they lead in a definite direction." He gestured toward where Vander's guards stood watch. "Get Huey and Louie and let's go. Following these is better than standing around with our dicks in our hand."

Gunnar whistled for the guards, and they flanked the back of their line as Jag led them through the trees and brush.

"What should we look for?" she whispered

to Damen as they walked.

He pointed toward the brush. "Snapped stalks or leaves on plants that have been broken or disturbed. The space between footprints. That can tell us a lot."

"Do you think it's an animal? A talking primate?" she asked. "Seems kind of farfetched."

Gunnar laughed, glancing at Henley. "Says the Earth woman on a distant planet with two shifter lovers."

She smirked, lifting a hand to his arm. "Point taken."

They walked for what seemed like forever, heading deeper and deeper into the foliage. Thick tree cover blocked the sun, and the insects swarmed, buzzing loudly. Henley swiped at them, but there were always more.

"Goddamned bugs!" she complained. "It's like we're a hot lunch for mosquitos or whatever these flying bloodsuckers are."

Damen paused, tapping Gunnar on the shoulder. He lifted his hand for the others to stop, but also lifted a finger to his lips. He motioned to Gunnar, pointing about fifty feet from the trail.

There was a fork in the almost non-existent path where a tree grew black as pitch. Its trunk reminded Henley of the mangroves on Earth, where the roots spiral together. The tree's canopy grew only one way, as if a non-existent wind forced the branches and leaves in that direction.

"I remember this," Gunnar whispered. "This is where we made camp that first night."

Damen nodded. "At that abandoned encampment." He looked around. "I remember the path here being very clear, though. Well-marked."

"Me too," he agreed. "Still, it's been a long time."

Jag pushed past them slightly, and looked at the tree and the surrounding area. "Do you two think you could find where the encampment was? Even if it's overgrown? There doesn't seem to be much in terms of signs of life. Was it that way when you first came?"

Damen shook his head. "No, just the opposite in fact."

"Let us take the lead. We'll scout things out ahead if you stay with Henley," Gunnar replied.

Damen shook his head again, this time disagreeing. "I'm usually one for divide and conquer, but I'd rather not split up. My gut is burning and I have that same heaviness in my chest as I had that first time in the jungle. I don't know how I know, but we're being watched."

"We all go, then." Gunnar nodded. "If I learned anything from that misguided trip, it was to trust Damen's instincts."

They pushed through the overgrowth, Gunnar swinging a curved machete-like weapon that sliced through vines and branches like butter. Damen had one across his back as well, and if the trail was wider, would have done the same.

Damen pointed for them to bear right, and soon enough Gunnar stopped, holding the blade high for everyone to halt. There ahead was a cold encampment. It wasn't abandoned or overgrown like the trail or the trading post. It was inhabited. Just empty as if the dwellers that had disappeared into the forest.

"I told you we were being watched," Damen said.

No sooner had the words left his mouth than painted warriors emerged from the foliage like ghosts. Damen and Gunnar exchanged a look. The men were painted, just as they remembered. They had found the Hatun.

Or the Hatun had found them.

SEVENTEEN

One of the men stepped ahead of the others. He carried a spear decorated with feathers and bones. More ceremonial that weapon. His headdress told them he was of importance, and Jag stepped ahead of the others to meet him halfway.

"You are trespassing," the principal man said, clearly stunning Jag and the others in their group that he spoke their language. "Surprised? We may look like savages, but only to uphold necessary traditions."

Damen stepped forward to flank Jag. "Traditions? Don't you mean necessary sacrifices?"

"You dare come into our territory and point fingers at our shaman?" The man who spoke was clearly a captain or a leader among the warriors. "Our holy man may be willing to hear what you have to say, but I'd as soon kill you where you stand."

Provoked, the line of warriors moved to flank their shaman, but the holy man raised his hand, stopping them in their tracks. "It's not our custom to be insulted on our own land. I will forgive your ill-mannered words. It is clear you know nothing of what you speak."

Gunnar moved to stand beside Damen, shaking his head. "We meant no disrespect, but we *do* know. Many years ago we were exploring this very forest, and made camp here our first night. The site was deserted, or at least it seemed to be, but we made use of the fire pits and lean-tos for the night. By our second night, the jungle seemed to close in, and we lost our way. We made camp in a clearing, only to witness something unspeakable."

The painted men exchanged looks, but their shaman kept his eyes on Gunnar. "What was it you saw?"

Damen explained, and the look on the shaman's face spoke volumes. Damon said, "We have since discovered a traitor to our king and our people that sold our women to be used in the same unspeakable way. Their betrayal was in exchange for poisons native to this land. Native to the Hatun."

The painted warriors moved to surround

Damen and Gunnar, who had stepped ahead of Jag. One warrior stalked forward, club in hand. "You know nothing of the suffering we have endured! What we still endure!"

"Enough!" the shaman demanded. "I will hear what these men have to say. If what they say is true and their women were taken against their will without the blessings of their families, we will talk more. If not, the woman with them will feed the Unduru when the moon rises tomorrow night."

The shaman dropped his hand, but one of their women cried out, rushing past him.

"No!" The warrior captain reached to stop her, but she twisted from his grip, moving to stand at the center between the factions.

"The women here know you speak the truth. We cared for your women until one by one they faced their deaths. They were taken against their will. Our women have suffered the same fate for generations. Not one mother willingly gave up her daughter, but for the Hatun there is no escape from the Unduru."

Damen's eyes softened at the pain in the woman's face. "I'm sorry for you, truly, but whatever deal Maddox made with your elders is over. The King of Galaxa knows everything. He's sent us to try and help, but if you resist and insist on continuing your sacrifices, then you leave us

MILLLY TAIDEN

no choice. The king will see you as a threat and have you destroyed."

Fists clenched, the woman took a step forward and raised her chin. "Send your warriors then. Oblivion is better than this living death. The women of this tribe live in terror. We bleed and we die. We cried for your women. Maybe if your king kills us, the Unduru will starve and die and the world will be safe."

"No!" Henley pushed past the men. "That's just it. The Unduru won't die. Not unless we work together to kill them. The king has scribes and archives and we know the stories and the legends. We know how to blast them from the face of Galaxa."

The shaman shook his head. "You think we don't have legends and histories? What you ask is impossible. You're asking me to send my people to their deaths."

"Isn't that what you're doing now, one at a time?" Henley asked.

The captain lifted his weapon and pointed it at Jag. "Control your woman or we'll control her for you!"

"First off, she's not my woman, but I doubt her mates could control her any more than you or I." Jag replied with a smirk. "The women of the Palladia are not subservient, nor are they fodder

173

for sacrifices. They are intelligent, strong and respected, as well as loved." He glanced to the lone woman standing between them and then to others standing in the back before looking to the captain again. "Don't you honor and revere your women? Or at least want the chance to?"

One by one, the warriors passed their captain to stand in a line, nodding. The shaman saw the expectant faces on their men and nodded as well. "We will hear what you have to say." He beckoned them toward a barricaded structure made of heavy wood and seamless joists.

The holy man stood in the entry offering a blessing as they each entered. The warrior captain was the last to enter the structure, closing the door. A heavy bolt stayed unlocked, and Damen raised an eyebrow.

"This is obviously a safe house for your people. You emerged earlier from the shadows as if taking shelter from something. Since you outnumber us five to one, why leave the door left bolted now?" he asked.

The shaman lifted a dismissive hand. "We are in no danger tonight."

He walked away without elaborating and Damen looked at Gunnar. "What the hell did he mean by that?"

"Look at the woman to his left." He gestured

with his chin to the woman's red, tear-swollen eyes. "That's why. Someone she loved was the most recent offering."

Damen took Henley by the hand and settled her between him and Gunnar. Jag took the lead as the royal representative while their guards flanked them on either side. Low cushions were spread around the inside of the structure, and tables dotted the places in between, loaded with food and drink.

The shaman sat at the head of the room, nodding for the others to do the same. "You are our honored guests," he said, but a sideways look to the captain put a time limit on their hospitality.

"No one knows where the Unduru came from or when they first inhabited the Tempera. Histories teach that the creatures once lived outside, taking shelter from the hot suns in the darkest parts of the jungle. They were the living dead that melted into the trees and attacked our village by night. Our ancestors found that sunlight was the only weapon that could be used against the Unduru. But the creatures are intelligent, and soon moved to a place where no sun exists."

Damen nodded. "Underground. We've heard this too. We also know that they are most vulnerable in the hour or so before dawn. That their strength leaves them and they walk in a dreamlike haze."

"Yes, but their lair is so deep in the Tempera caverns, no light can penetrate," the captain replied.

Jag looked at them, curious. "What if we were to lure them to the surface? Or if not to the surface, than close enough we could find a way to expose them to light."

"Or fire." Henley interjected, and everyone turned. "We have our own legends on Earth. Your living dead creatures aren't that different from ours, except for the nasty worms in their gut. Fire can render them helpless, and then snap—" she snapped her fingers. "We go in and behead the bastards and drive a stake through their hearts just because." She nodded, grinning.

The captain of the warriors laughed, raising an eyebrow. "You weren't kidding about Palladian women."

Jag smiled, lifting a hand Henley's way. "Beautiful *and* daring."

"...And ours," Gunnar added as Damen nodded.

"So," Jag continued. "What do you think? You obviously know the location of the Unduru lair, or at least have a good idea. We could set out at first light and strike at noon when the sun reaches its peak and take them down for good."

The holy man stood, motioning for the others to do the same. "It's late. We both have much to think on, so let's speak again before dawn. You are welcome to stay the night in our lodge. No harm will come to you here. This is a scared space."

His gut churning again, Damen caught the look between the warrior captain and one of his men as they left the building. "I'm not so sure about the no-harm thing. We need to keep an eye out. I'll take the first watch."

EIGHTEEN

Gunnar turned over on his bedroll, coughing. He opened his eyes to thick smoke swirling around them in the lodge as fire climbed the wooden walls, igniting the beams above them.

"Shit! Get up!" He scrambled to his feet, keeping low to breathe. He coughed again, trying to yell. "The building's on fire! We have to get out, *now!*"

Gunnar shook Damen's shoulder, before crawling to wake everyone else. "C'mon! We gotta go!" He helped Henley to her feet. "Stay low, babe. It's bad." He rooted for a scarf he saw near one of the lamps, handing it to her to cover her mouth and nose.

She followed close behind as he made his way through the smoke. "Is the door still unlocked, you think?"

"I hope so or we're fucked." Damen coughed, eyes streaming.

Gunnar reached for the handle, but pulled his hand back with a hiss. "Fuck! It's red hot! What now?"

"We have to go through. It's the only way out," Damen said, pulling his sleeve down over his palm. "Take Henley and I'll try to break the latch!"

Jag pushed passed him and threw his shoulder at the heavy door. The wood splintered and wisps of fresh, cool air seeped through the cracks. The blaze behind them surged at the influx of oxygen.

"Shit! Stupid. Stupid. Stupid!" Jag scowled, shielding his face.

Henley took the scarf from her face and handed it to Jag. "Use this!" she nodded.

He wrapped the knit material around his hand and gripped the red hot handle, hissing as he lifted the latch. The five of them staggered into the dark, sucking in deep gulps.

The Hatun raced toward them, woven buckets in hand. They formed a line from their well, throwing bucketful after bucketful to put out the flames.

Coughing, Henley staggered toward a tree far enough from the flames. Damen called after her, but she shook her head. "I'm fine. Go help the others."

He hesitated, but watched as she slumped against the base of the trunk, still waving him off. He jogged back to the fire, but Gunnar grabbed his arm as he joined the line.

"Where's Henley?" he asked. "She okay?"

He jerked his thumb toward the tree across from the commotion. "She's fine. She's resting..." he glanced over his shoulder toward where he last saw her, but she was gone.

"Fuck!" He turned on his heel and raced to where she'd been only moments ago with Gunnar close behind.

Damen's eyes searched the perimeter. "She was just here! Maybe she went into one of the huts."

His eyes caught one of the Hatun warriors staggering from the edge of the woods. He ran to the man, his eyes narrowing when he saw Henley's dagger protruding from his shoulder just above his heart.

"Where is she? What have you done with her?" Damen ripped the dagger from the man's shoulder, forcing him to the ground.

Gunner picked up Henley's blade from the ground, his face hard and feral. A growl ripped from his throat as he hauled the man up by his neck, lifting him until his feet dangled.

"You'd better answer, boy, or I'll rip you to shreds in front of your own." Gunnar shook the Hatun until the young man's teeth rattled in his mouth.

The shaman rushed over with his captain to where Gunnar and Damen stood, eyes flaming red. Razor claws, sharp enough to cut through skin and bone, pushed through Damen's fingertips. His roar echoed through the Tempera forests, silencing the night.

Gunnar sniffed the man's hands as he dangled terrified. "He started the fire. The scent of it is all over his hands."

"How can you be so sure?" the shaman accused.

Damen turned blood-red eyes on the holy man. "You would know the answer to that if you were shifters. We can smell the acrid oils on the traitor's fingers, but that's nothing compared to the scent of fear pouring from his skin. He's guilty, but he's not alone."

"Surely, you don't suspect me!" the holy man balked.

"No, but I know the identity of his accomplice. His scent is as clear as yours and mine." Gunnar looked at Damen.

Gunnar turned his eyes to the Hatun

shaman. "The stunned look on your face tells me you were betrayed, but your captain's face tells a different story. His scent is bitter with fear right now. No wonder he drew such a hard line when we came into your camp last night."

The captain sprang forward, a dagger in his hand, but Damen sliced the captain's wrist with a single slash, severing the hand holding the dagger from the rest of his arm.

The captain screamed, cradling the stump in his other hand. Jag ran over with Vander's guard, surrounding the shaman. The holy man held out his fingers, crooking them in the air as if squeezing something invisible. "If you value your family and their lives you will tell us everything you know. Where is the bears' woman?"

The captain's eyes bugged as he struggled for breath, his face red, then purple before the shaman released his grip. The captain dropped to his knees at the same time Gunnar dropped his henchman. The two knelt, shaking in front of Gunnar and Damen as well as their shaman.

"Forgive me," the young Hatun begged. "I was forced."

The captain hissed, but he couldn't help the sneer on his face amid the pain. "Forced? You would have fucked the woman before delivering her to Naz Voda if she didn't stab you first!"

Damen roared again, his clawed hand slicing the young Hatun's throat to his backbone with one swipe. The man gurgled once before he crumpled to the ground in a spreading pool of blood.

The captain's eyes went wide and he swallowed, his hand moving to his throat. "It was Naz Voda. He faked his death so he could continue his flesh trade with us. He…he's behind this. Not me."

"Where is he and where did he take Henley?" Gunnar's voice growled.

The captain bowed his head, his hands shaking as he pointed toward the west. "The pit."

Jag looked at the shaman. "Do you know what he means?"

The holy man nodded. "Yes. A fissure in the side of a small craggy rise. It leads to a set of three caves with only one entrance. It is where the Unduru sleep."

Gunnar's hand shot out grabbing the captain by the throat, but the shaman reached out a tentative hand. "You've taken the life of one Hatun already. This one is mine to deal with."

With a nod, Gunnar released his hold, but no sooner had the captain dragged in a breath, then the holy man magically squeezed the life out of him with the whole of the tribe as witness. The captain released a death gasp and then fell forward, dead eyes staring into nothing.

The shaman turned to his people and lifted his hand. "My magic and our people have been tainted by two traitors. We will do whatever we can to help retrieve our guests, save their mate, and maybe even destroy the Unduru." His eyes matched every gaze surrounding them as they stood with the remnants of their safe house still smoking. "The fire is out and we will rebuild, but now we move. Daylight is breaking."

The shaman walked toward his people to prepare, leaving Damen, Gunnar, and Jag standing alone.

"I'm going to rip Naz Voda limb from limb and leave him for the buzzards," Damen growled.

Gunnar shook his head. "Not if I get to him first."

NINETEEN

The shaman led a small group of Hatun warriors through the jungle. Sunlight streamed through the trees, glistening on the still damp leaves. There were signs everywhere of a struggle and Gunnar's chest tightened. Drag marks were evident in the soft ground and snapped twigs and scarred roots showed Henley had gone kicking and fighting.

"If she's dead, I'm going to go postal on this place," Damen ground out.

Gunnar looked at him, confused. "Postal? I don't know what that means, but if it sounds the way I think it sounds, I'm with you, bro."

Jaw tight, Damen eyed both his alpha and the prince. "It means no one but us and ours leaves here alive if Henley's life force has gone from her body."

"Agreed," Jag murmured.

They trekked for what seemed like forever until they came to a clearing where the ground was black with years of blood.

"Is this the clearing you remember?" Jag asked.

Damen nodded, fists clenched.

Gunnar put his hand on his shoulder and squeezed. "Inhale. Henley wasn't kept here. She passed through, but wasn't restrained."

"I know, but my gut is roiling and not from my own anger. We're walking into a trap. I can feel it," Damen replied.

Jag eyed the shaman. "Then we go in with our guide leading the way and claws ready to rip his heart out through his back."

They crossed a water barrier. Not a coursing river like they found at the edge of the trading post, but big enough they needed to wade across single file. Once across, the terrain sloped upward. Pictograms carved into large boulders were clear warnings, telling them they were close.

The trees grew taller, their trunks massive and winding as they arched together blocking out the sun. It was as if darkness had wiped the day from the sky, with only small slivers of light piercing the gloom.

The cloister of trees led straight to a rock face that seems to erupt from the ground out of nowhere. At the center was a crevice twice the width of a man. Jag motioned for the shaman to go first.

"You lead. If Naz Voda sees you first, he'll question you while he decides whether or not to slit your throat. It will give us time to assess," Jag said.

Gunnar shot him a look. "Nice, why not give the old man even more incentive to roll over on us."

The shaman lifted his chin. "I will do what is necessary to protect my people. Our women are right. We cannot live in fear any more. So many have been sacrificed already, if it means my life now, then my debt to the universe will be paid."

He inhaled and stepped through the slot in the rock face, waiting as the others followed. The interior opened to a wide, sand-bottomed hollow that seemed carved from the inside out. Tall pillars hewn from the same thick sandstone supported the ceiling, yet pebbles crumbled from the sides despite the braces.

The smell of old blood filled their noses, and Gunnar winced at the stench. Husks of dead worms and larvae cluttered the base of the interior walls, brown stains from their slime coating the sand in spots. A woman whimpered and all eyes jerked ahead.

"Henley?" Jag mouthed, and Gunnar inhaled, his face like stone as he nodded.

Damen pointed toward the direction of the cry and they progressed in quiet stealth. They moved quickly and were three-quarters through the hollow when Gunnar spied an inner cave. It wasn't very large and partially obscured.

"The entire place is carved from the inside out," Gunnar noted. "No sun and nothing to burn in here. What do we do when we find Henley? How do we get out of here alive?"

Jag pulled the small but lethal weapon from his waistband before securing it again. "I know we said no fusion weapons, but you gave Henley a dagger, and thank the gods you did. I brought this for insurance, and it looks like we might need it after all. This place doesn't look too secure, so when I blast the ceiling wide open, be prepared to duck and run. One flash from this little baby and the Unduru will see their lair in a whole new light, if you know what I mean." He winked.

Damen grinned, giving Gunnar a quick look. "The palace rule breaker."

"Why not?" Gunnar nodded, agreeing.

Another cry in the dark and they shut up. Gunnar inhaled, and his faced paled. "She's bleeding. Not new injuries, but enough to spark interest for the Unduru. She's here somewhere. We've gotta find her."

"How very astute, Gunnar. I guess there's a reason they pay the alpha the big bucks with a beauty like this one." Naz Voda walked from the mouth of the small cave, dragging Henley behind him.

With a practiced move, he lifted a bamboo shoot to his mouth, sending two darts into Vander's guards. The men dropped where they stood, dead, and he laughed. "Two down, three to go. Shame I only had two poison darts in my pocket."

"Let me go, you asshole!" Henley fought, trying to jerk him off balance, but the rough rope where Naz Voda tied her wrists and her feet, cut into already raw abrasions.

Damen bent to attack. "Let her go, Voda! You're outnumbered and you know it."

Naz drew a blade upward, holding the sharp tip to Henley's throat. "I don't think so, brother bear."

Henley's breath hitched and her body tensed, her panic sending Damen and Gunnar's eyes flashing red.

"I suggest you give your primal urges another think, boys. One quick slice and the Unduru won't be able to resist. They will swarm at the scent of fresh blood and we'll all die." Naz laughed, turning to the shaman and his men, taunting them as well. "Your people are going to have to pay in blood for your betrayal, holy man. You should have let your captain handle things instead of sticking your nose where it doesn't belong."

The shaman raised his chin. "The Hatun have already paid in blood. As for my captain, he got what was coming to him as will you." He lifted his hand, crooking his fingers into a claw as he did with the captain, but Naz Voda laughed in his face.

"I'm part shifter, holy man. Your magic doesn't work on us," Naz sneered.

Gunnar eyed the man, ready to kill. "*Us*?" he questioned. "You're no shifter, Naz Voda. You're broken. Two shifter parents and not one drop of shifter ability."

"Wait…" Damen laughed, but there was no humor in the sound. "Are you saying he's a scratch?"

Naz Voda stared him down, but Damen laughed even harder. "Maybe we should get a shifter female to bite him in the ass. That way the loser might stand a chance."

The man's face twisted and he jerked Henley toward the closest pillar. "You won't be laughing much longer, bear boy. Not once I lash your mate to a post and slice her from cunt to throat."

He put the knife in his teeth to grab the ends of Henley's ropes, and that was the only opening needed. Damen crouched, his back arching as his eyes flared red. Gunnar's arms thickened and his shoulders bulged, his eyes flashing crimson as well.

Naz Voda shoved Henley against the column, her head snapping back. "Give it a rest, Gunnar. What do you and your playmate think your lumbering asses can do so far away from the ice and snow? Your claws and teeth can't do much if you can't catch me. I'll slit her throat and disappear before you heavy weights can plod your way across."

"I can help with that," Jag's voice slurred through his fangs as his body ripped and reshaped. In seconds, an enormous ancient cat sprang from massive hind legs, knocked Naz Voda to the ground away from Henley. He howled, turning his big head to Gunnar and Damen. It was their turn.

The shaman raised his hands and clapped once, beginning a low chant. The sound grew until it echoed from the cavern walls. Dripping water, clinked to the ground in ice pellets. Along the walls and floor, thick condensation froze to sheets of ice.

The Hatun ran for cover, racing the spreading frost, hiding as Damen and Gunnar crouched, their bodies twisting as muscle and sinew tore and reformed. Sleek white fur replaced skin and heavy limbs replaced arms and legs. Lethal, scythed claws dug into the ice-covered ground as razor-edged teeth dripped with the need to kill.

Naz Voda screamed as he scrambled to his feet, his cry reverberating in the hollow room, sending chunks of ice and rock crumbling from the ceiling and walls. He slipped and fell, landing in front of Jag's front paws. With a chuff, the big cat batted him across the slick ground.

Naz Voda slid like an offering toward both bears. Damen caught the man's shoulder in one massive paw. Razor-edged claws dug into his flesh as the snow bear stood, lifting the man twelve feet as he straightened to his full height.

Eyes wide with fear, Voda watched Gunnar approach. There was no quick swipe severing the jugular. Gunnar and Damen each took a leg ripping each from his body. He screamed as they tore his belly open, before ripping his arms from his sides, leaving his head for last. Their white fur was smeared red with blood, and the scent of a fresh kill sent the sand floor to rumble.

The Unduru were awake.

Jag shifted back to a man and quickly untied

Henley. Weak but determined, she picked up Naz Voda's blade and turned toward the cave's entrance.

"Hen, we gotta go," Jag urged. "We can't fight them, much as I'd love to. Nature has to do this with a little help from us, but you need to take cover."

She tore her eyes from the cave entrance, taking in Jag's naked frame. "Speaking of cover, I think we'd better get you a fig leaf or Riley's going to kick my ass when we get back to the palace."

Damen and Gunnar shifted quickly as well. They grabbed Henley, shoving her toward the shaman as Jag yelled for the Hatun to leave as well. Hideous creatures with gaping maws and knife-edge teeth shuffled from the cave's depths, their reek of death and rotted flesh preceding them. Their enormous eyes tracked the darkness. They were taller than the shifters, with gray emaciated skin stretched over bones.

They seemed to move as though in a dreamlike haze, and Gunnar nudged Damen's arm. "They smell the blood, but they're still affected by the time of day," he whispered.

Damen scrambled for his pack and pulled his fusion laser from the side pouch. "It's noon and that means lunchtime, so who are we to keep them waiting." He pointed his laser at the ceiling, but then hesitated, watching Gunnar reach for his pack, as well. The alpha unzipped the center compartment, pulling out two more weapons, tossing one to Jag.

"Okay," Damen said, flipping the safety off. "Let's lock and load."

"The palace rule breaker, huh." Jag cracked a grin, as the alpha and omega triangulated their positions with his.

They each aimed for the ceiling. Rapid fire beams blasted the ice and rock point blank, the heat from the lasers scorching the stone on contact. The ceiling rumbled, falling in chunks to the ground. The rock exploded, breaking into rubble, crushing some of the Unduru.

Aiming again, their lasers incinerated the trees and roots above, the fiery explosion. A wide swath of sunlight bathed the inner chamber in bright light. The Unduru screamed as their flesh blackened and split before erupting into flame. Worms fled from their split guts, popping and sizzling one by one. The Unduru were dead by nature's hand with a little help from laser fusion.

The stench was almost unbearable, and Gunnar wiped his streaming eyes. "What if there are more still lurking in the dark below?" he asked.

Jag pulled his pack from under a pile of

rubble, wincing at the charred smell that permeated the room. He unzipped the side and pulled out a small, egg shaped weapon.

"Is that what I think it is?" Gunnar asked.

Nodding, Jag tossed it to him. "Do the honors, dude, and let's go home. I've been away from my mate for too long."

Gunnar pulled the pin on the UV bomb and threw it deep into the heart of the cavern below. They turned on their heels, and hightailed it through the hollow, slipping through the crevice to take cover.

The explosion shook the Tempera, but there was no smoke. Only the dust from crumbling rock and a satisfying sizzle that told them the Unduru were no more.

TWENTY

"You sure there are no more of those gross creatures?" Ivy asked, shifting the baby to her other breast beneath her nursing blanket.

Damen nodded. "As far as we know, they're toast courtesy of our dual suns and the latest laser technology."

"What about those poor people," Riley asked, struggling for their name. "The Hatun?"

Henley exhaled a snort. "Poor people? Honey, you forget they were the ones who went all primitive on their own people, sacrificing their women to those gross creatures. They were the ones who struck a deal with Maddox and Naz Voda to traffic in our gals. I can only imagine what was next in Maddox's sick mind. Probably slave transports from Earth or some other planet."

Damen picked up his glass of Sidaii wine and lifted it in salute. "We won't have to worry about that or *him* much longer. I personally gave him a dose of his own medicine. Literally."

Vander nodded with a satisfied smirk. "True dat, to quote my beautiful mate. The man is writhing as we speak, and we made sure he knew before we administered the poison. Of course, we'll burn his body afterward just to be sure it's purified. As to those 'poor people' —" the king crooked his fingers, "I have to believe they thought they had no choice. Before Jag left the Tempera, I asked him to invite the Hatun and their shaman to speak with our council, though I think it would be a good idea to send a contingent back to the jungle with extra UV weapons just to do a second sweep."

"Agreed," Jag said, slipping into a chair in the direct sun. "I for one am not a fan of closed dark places anymore."

Riley shuddered, sliding onto Jag's lap with a glass of Sidaii wine. "Me too! We are sleeping with a UV light on from now on. The stories Henley told us gave me the permanent heebie-jeebies."

He took the wine glass from her hand and drained the cup before planting a kiss on her cheek. "You're not the only one, babe, but the Hatun are bringing the antidote for the worm poison along with the ingredients so our labs can research their chemical makeup."

Henley nodded, leaning her head on Damen's shoulder as she sat between him and Gunnar. "It's funny how poisons and their medicinal antidotes come from the jungle here as well as on Earth. Must be the climate or the teeming vegetation."

"Ugh, not to mention the bugs," Riley shuddered again. "No thanks. I think I'll leave the adventuring to you, Hen. My kids are enough of an undertaking."

Gunnar smiled. "You all have nothing to worry about. As far as the Hatun and their monsters are concerned, Maddox isn't the only thing being purified, and his black market route is closed. When we get back to the Summit, the first rule of business will be shutting down any and all black market trade for good."

"We?" Ivy asked, raising an eyebrow.

He nodded, but spared a glance for Damen to explain.

"I already spoke to Vander, but you all should know as well. I'm returning to the Summit with Gunnar. It's time."

"But this is your home," she protested. "You're our security chief and an important member of this family. You're Uncle Damen to our kids."

He smiled at the queen. "Don't think of it as me deserting, Ivy. My leaving is fulfilling my destiny. Besides, it'll give you an excuse to escape the desert heat and us an escape from the cold when we visit back and forth."

Henley got up and switched seats to sit beside Gerri. "You're very quiet. That's not like you. Aren't you happy with the way your plan worked out? Win-win, right?"

A slow smile spread on the matchmaker's lips and she shrugged. "I love a happy ending, dear, but there's still part of this story yet to be told." She took Henley's cheeks in both her hands and inhaled. The older woman's slow smile spread to a full grin. "I knew it!"

Henley's mouth dropped open. "You couldn't. I just…I mean…"

"What are you two mumbling about?" Damen asked, raising an eyebrow. "That knowing look on Gerri's face always means trouble."

The matchmaker let go of Henley's cheeks, sticking her tongue out in reply. "I never bring trouble. I may shake things up and push people out of their comfort zones, but it always works out for the best. My track record is one hundred percent."

"So," Gunnar looked between the two women. "Are you going to answer the question or should we just guess?"

Henley looked between Gunnar and Damen, sparing a glance for Gerri before a slow smile took her face as well. "After we got back from the Tempera, you two insisted I have my wounds looked at by the doctor. He ran all kinds of test to make sure I hadn't been infected by the Unduru while Naz Voda held me hostage."

"Yes, and he told us you were fine," Damen replied. "And for the record, I never want to speak that asshole's name again, okay?"

Henley shot him a smirk, but lifted a hand to continue. "Anyway, the doctor did find something. Turns out I have a condition that absolutely requires we visit back and forth."

Worry and fear immediately creased both Damen and Gunnar's faces. "What?" Damen asked. "Whatever you need, you got it. We'll import doctors to the Summit if necessary."

"Nope, not necessary, Uncle Damen, but the transport back and forth will be, that is if we want *our* baby to know their *cousins*."

Ivy handed the baby to Vander and wiggled her boobs back into her bra. "Wait. Are you saying what I think you're saying?"

Henley nodded. "Yes! I'm going to have a

baby!"

Riley and Ivy were practically airborne to the couch, jumping up and down, squealing. Ivy exhaled, and looked over her shoulder at Vander. "From now on there's to be a Summit shuttle just for us to use whenever we want, okay?"

He chuckled, nodding. "Whatever you say, babe."

Henley peeled her friends from her neck, her eyes searching Gunnar and Damen's faces. "Are you guys okay with this?" she asked, getting up from her spot next to Gerri. "You're both a little too calm for comfort."

"Is the doctor sure, Hen?" Damen asked. "It's only been a couple weeks."

Gunnar nudged his omega's arm. "What this bonehead is trying to say is we're over the moon about it, that is if it's really real."

Gerri chuckled. "For two intelligent shifters, you two are pretty dense. Either that or frying those gross creatures has damaged your sense of smell. Take a whiff. Henley is most definitely preggers, but even the doctors can't know what I do."

"What?" Henley asked, both curious and concerned.

The matchmaker grinned. "I know for certain your triad is going to be increased by *two*, not one."

Henley whirled on her feet. "Twins?"

"Yup." She nodded in reply. "Twins. A boy and a girl. Each fathered by one of your mates."

Henley shook her head, floored. "How can you possibly know that?"

"Haven't you all learned anything yet?" Gerri tapped the side of her head. "I know, because I *know*." She got up and gave Henley a tight hug before taking her by the hand and walking her back to her mates. "Dual suns. Dual-natures. Dual mates. It's almost as if it were written."

Damen pulled Henley down between him and Gunnar and they each kissed her cheeks. "Well," he said, letting his fingers trail her bare arm. "There's only one thing left to do."

Gunnar nodded. "But we need to get home, first."

TWENTY-ONE

"Hey, you two realize I'm pregnant with twins, right?" Henley huffed as they headed up the slope toward a cabin carved into the highest point on the summit.

Damen scooped her into his arms, settling her in all her furs against his chest. "Well, you were the one who didn't want to take the alpacas."

"Nooo, thanks. I'd rather be a sweat ball when we get to the cabin than risk a sore ass or a miscarriage from those walking carpets bouncing me around like a ragdoll."

Damen laughed. "If it makes you feel better, I much prefer this mode of travel. Your scent was intoxicating before, but now? My dick is so hard, I can barely keep it in my pants."

"Hey, you two, get a move on!" Gunnar

called from fifty yards ahead. "I'm going to get the fire going. Hurry up!" They watched him sprint the rest of the way to the cabin.

Henley sighed. "I was hoping I could be a shifter, like Riley and Ivy, but I'll be a walking balloon belly soon, so that's out."

"What makes you say that?" Damen asked, picking up the pace to double time it up the slope. "Anything's possible now that you're ours." He hesitated for a moment. "You are ours, right? You've decided. This is your home, now. *We* are your home."

She nodded, giving his lips a peck. "Yes, Damen. For the hundredth time."

"Good." He stepped up on the porch and let her slide down his full hard length.

Henley straightened her clothes, dusting the snow from her hair and shoulders as Damen opened the door. She walked through the doors and looked at the cozy surroundings. Bright polished wood and hewn beams made the cabin almost a miniature of the grand Summit lodge. It was homey, though. Perfect for a weekend getaway for three.

"The mountains can get a little nippy this time of year," he said as she shivered near the door.

"Nippy? It's fucking frigid! And speaking

of nips, this weather is making mine pucker like they're ready to rip through my shirt!" she grinned.

His eyes darkened. "And here I thought it was being against me making your tits ache." Pulling her closer, he pressed his lips against her hair before turning her around to walk her backwards toward the couch and the fire Gunnar already had blazing.

Gunnar met them at the large, wide sofa, and took her hand, a gorgeous seductive grin on his mouth. "Maybe you need a little friction to warm you up. A soft place to spread yourself by the fire."

"Soft place." She laughed. "You two are as hard as calculus."

Slipping in behind her, Gunnar peeled her fur coat from her shoulders, tossing it to the floor on the opposite side of the couch. He reached around and lifted her sweater, dragging it over her head as well.

"Braless," Damen grinned, his eyes darkening. "Seems like anticipation was the reason your nipples were hard."

Gunnar slid his hands from her waist to cup her breasts from behind. He grazed over her stiff peaks, rolling her nipples between his thumb and forefinger.

She inhaled, leaning back against Gunnar's chest, her arch jutting her breasts higher into his hands.

Damen cupped her pussy through her leggings. "And you, my love, are dripping already, and I plan to pound your pretty pink cunt until you scream for release."

Her eyes met his grin with a teasing smile of her own. "On my knees or straddled?"

"Woman, either way. It's just us on this lonely mountaintop, so strip. This is a no clothes zone for the next three days," Gunnar answered, slipping his hands from her breasts to hook the top of her waistband.

She stepped back from them, knowing they watched every move. Kicking off her fur-lined boots, she moved back barefooted, rolling her leggings down in a sexy swivel before kicking them off her ankles. She stood naked, except for a black lace thong.

"Oh, babe, you look good enough to eat." Gunnar licked his lips.

Henley tapped her chin, lifting her head so her high ponytail brushed her back. "I was thinking the same thing about you two, and since this is a no clothes zone, you two are in clear violation." She reached up and freed her hair, letting it tumble to her bare breasts.

Damen shed his clothes, tossing them to the side. Gunnar did the same, and the two moved to flank her on either side. It was her turn to lick her lips at the hard, corded lengths pressed against her soft flesh.

Gunnar moved her hair from her shoulder and kissed her neck while his fingers reached between her legs to stroke her pussy through her panties.

"These are so sexy," he said, slipping his fingers beneath the top band. "I hope you brought more with you."

"Why?" she asked, her breath catching as he grazed her clit through the lace.

The delicate fabric popped as he tore the thong from her hips and gently slipped it from her body. "That's why," he answered, spreading her exposed pussy lips.

"I would have taken them off, you know," her voice hitched as he grazed her bare clit.

Damen's hands slipped around to her breasts. "What's the fun in that?" he said, working her nipples as his mouth teased her throat.

"Spread your legs, love," Gunnar asked, and when Henley did, he knelt dipping his face between her thighs. His tongue flicked her hard nub as high hands spread her pussy wider, drawing the nub between his lips.

Henley sucked in a breath as he pulled back to slip his fingers into her wet cleft. "Come, love," he said, licking her clit again. "I want you so wet, your cunt sucks my cock so deep my balls tremble with the need shoot my load. Do you want that? My hard dick stuffing your cunt while Damen stuffs your ass?"

Her breath caught, and she was barely able to croak, let alone give a coherent answer. Not that she could with Damen claiming her mouth. He sucked her tongue and plundered her mouth, their breath mingling.

Gunnar pulled his hand from her, licking her juice from her fingers. "I want you so hot and wet, you beg for my cock, beg for my hot jets deep inside you — beg for Damen's deep in your ass. Then you'll be ready."

This was it. They wanted her and she wanted them. There was no going back from this point. She gasped at the feel of their hands on her body. No going back. She couldn't even if she tried. She was ready.

"Time to ride the wave, baby," Damen whispered over her mouth. He dragged her bottom lip through his teeth and Henley hissed as he pinched her nipples.

Gunnar licked her engorged pussy, sucking

and teasing as her juice ran over his chin from her waiting sex. "You like it hard and thick," he teased. "The way we fill you front and back."

Henley moaned against Damen's mouth, but he broke their kiss. "My turn," he whispered and switched places with Gunnar. He dropped to his knees and spread her slick entrance wide, curling three fingers deep to her spot.

"Taste yourself on my tongue, love. Savor your sweet juice on my lips." Gunnar took her mouth and her scent was all over him as he kissed her. "You are so fucking sexy, Henley," he whispered. "Delicious."

Damen circled her spot, sucking her clit hard and fast, using his tongue to tease. Henley ripped her mouth from Gunnar's, her head dropping back onto his shoulder.

As she almost crested, Damen pulled his hand and his mouth away. "I know you love the feel of my mouth on your clit. Hot and hungry. But you can't love…not yet."

"Damen, please!"

"You want it bad, Henley?" Gunnar asked, nipping her ear. "How bad? Tell us how much you want our cocks."

She groaned trying to fist Damen's hair and push him back to her pussy, but he stood instead, his hands grazing her skin like static electricity. "No, baby." His fingers feathered across her belly and her breasts.

"We need to hear you," Gunnar said. "You have to say the words."

"Fuck me! Both of you! In my cunt. In my ass!" Her body burned with unspent need and she lifted her hands, to her hair. "Take me. Claim me. I'm yours!"

Damen pulled her down with him to the soft fur rug, the fire cracking behind them. He lay back on a pillow helping her straddle his hips. He teased her soft folds with his swollen head, slapping her clit with his cock as Gunnar's fingers spread her slick juice from her slit to her ass.

Gunnar pushed her cheeks wide. "Inch by inch, babe. I love watching your tight hole swallow my full length. Your face tense, wanting more." He dug his fingers into her soft flesh as his engorged head stretched her wide.

She hissed, and Damen fisted his corded cock against his belly, his other hand teasing her clit as Gunnar filled her ass. The alpha thrust deep and Henley took his full length with a gasp, but as he pulled back for a second thrust, Damen pressed his head to her wet, swollen pussy.

"Do it. Please!"

His eyes flashed dark and streaked and he plunged his cock into her wet cleft as Gunnar did the same in her ass. Her hips rocked as he drove his dick deeper and harder, a guttural growl leaving his throat.

She threw her head back, and Gunnar's hands fisted her hair as he thrust. Henley cried out at the feel of them inside her, her body tensed and ready. She rolled her hips, each roll grinding her ass back as both men thrust harder and faster until she screamed, her climax ripping through her body.

Claws pushed through Damen's fingers and his eyes rolled over gold and red. With a guttural yell, his dick pumped his release deep into her body, her walls milking every last drop from him with every spasm. He gripped her thigh, his claws scoring four even marks into her soft flesh.

Gunnar growled behind her ear, nipping the side of her neck before pulling back. He thrust one last time, his cock swelling deep in her ass as hot jets spurted in her tight hole. One hand held her shoulders and his fingers curled against her skin, sharp claws pushing through to slash her back behind her shoulder blade.

Henley hissed, but another climax shuddered through her body, taking every ounce of pain. She was theirs. A triad of love and lust. Now and for always.

EPILOGUE

Gerri was going back to earth. She smiled at the gifts piled in her room from her last three matches. She was so glad things had worked out for her hard-headed trio. Sadness tried to creep its way into her heart, but she pushed it away as she always did. Later, when she was alone, she'd think about her mate.

Now was not the time. There was a lot of work ahead of her and a brand new set of clients waiting for their mates. Good thing she loved to travel, because the upcoming trips were going to take her to places she hadn't visited in a long time.

ABOUT THE AUTHOR

New York Times and USA Today Bestselling Author

Hi! I'm Milly Taiden. I love to write sexy stories featuring fun, sassy heroines with curves and growly alpha males with fur. My books are a great way to satisfy your craving for contemporary or paranormal romance with action, humor, suspense and happily ever afters.

I live in Florida with my hubby, our boys, and our fur children Speedy, Stormy and our newest baby boy, Teddy. I am seriously addicted to chocolate and cake.

I love to meet new readers, so come sign up for my newsletter and check out my Facebook page. We always have lots of fun stuff going on there.

SIGN UP FOR MILLY'S NEWSLETTER FOR LATEST NEWS!

http://eepurl.com/pt9q1

Find out more about Milly Taiden here:

Email: millytaiden@gmail.com

Website: http://www.millytaiden.com

Instagram: http://www.instagram.com/millytaiden

Facebook:
http://www.facebook.com/millytaidenpage

Twitter: https://www.twitter.com/millytaiden

If you liked this story, you might also enjoy the following by Milly Taiden:

Sassy Mates / Sassy Ever After Series

Scent of a Mate *Book One*

A Mate's Bite *Book Two*

Unexpectedly Mated *Book Three*

A Sassy Wedding *Short 3.7*

The Mate Challenge *Book Four*

Sassy in Diapers *Short 4.3*

Fighting for Her Mate *Book Five*

A Fang in the Sass *Book 6*

Also, check out the **Sassy Ever After World on Amazon**

A.L.F.A Series

Elemental Mating *Book One*

Mating Needs *Book Two*

Dangerous Mating *Book Three (Coming Soon)*

Fearless Mating *Book Four (Coming Soon)*

Savage Shifters

Savage Bite *Book One*

Savage Kiss *Book Two*

Savage Hunger *Book Three*

Drachen Mates

Bound in Flames *Book One*

Bound in Darkness *Book Two*

Bound in Eternity *Book Three*

Bound in Ashes *Book Four*

Federal Paranormal Unit

Wolf Protector *Federal Paranormal Unit Book One*

Dangerous Protector *Federal Paranormal Unit Book Two*

Unwanted Protector *Federal Paranormal Unit Book Three*

Paranormal Dating Agency

Twice the Growl *Book One*

Geek Bearing Gifts *Book Two*

The Purrfect Match *Book Three*

Curves 'Em Right *Book Four*

Tall, Dark and Panther *Book Five*

The Alion King *Book Six*

There's Snow Escape *Book Seven*

Scaling Her Dragon *Book Eight*

In the Roar *Book Nine*

Scrooge Me Hard *Short One*

Bearfoot and Pregnant *Book Ten*

All Kitten Aside *Book Eleven*

Oh My Roared *Book Twelve*

Piece of Tail *Book Thirteen*

Kiss My Asteroid *Book Fourteen*

Scrooge Me Again *Short Two*

Born with a Silver Moon *Book Fifteen*

Sun in the Oven *Book Sixteen*

Between Ice and Frost *Book Seventeen (Coming Soon)*

Also, check out the **Paranormal Dating Agency World on Amazon**

Raging Falls

Miss Taken *Book One*

Miss Matched *Book Two*

Miss Behaved *Book Three*

Miss Behaved *Book Three*

Miss Mated *Book Four (Coming Soon)*

Miss Conceived *Book Five (Coming Soon)*

FUR-ocious Lust - Bears

Fur-Bidden *Book One*

Fur-Gotten *Book Two*

Fur-Given Book *Three*

FUR-ocious Lust - Tigers

Stripe-Tease *Book Four*

Stripe-Search *Book Five*

Stripe-Club *Book Six*

Night and Day Ink

Bitten by Night *Book One*

Seduced by Days *Book Two*

Mated by Night *Book Three*

Taken by Night *Book Four*

Dragon Baby *Book Five*

Shifters Undercover

Bearly in Control *Book One*

Fur Fox's Sake *Book Two*

Black Meadow Pack

Sharp Change *Black Meadows Pack Book One*

Caged Heat *Black Meadows Pack Book Two*

Other Works

Wolf Fever

Fate's Wish

Wynter's Captive

Sinfully Naughty Vol. 1

Don't Drink and Hex

Hex Gone Wild

Hex and Kisses

Alpha Owned

Match Made in Hell

Alpha Geek

HOWLS Romances

The Wolf's Royal Baby

Her Fairytale Wolf *Co-Written*

The Wolf's Dream Mate *Co-Written*

Her Winter Wolves *Co-Written*

Contemporary Works

Lucky Chase

Their Second Chance

Club Duo Boxed Set

A Hero's Pride

A Hero Scarred

A Hero for Sale

Wounded Soldiers Set

If you enjoyed the book, please consider leaving a review, even if it's only a line or two; it would make all the difference and would be very much appreciated.

Thank you!

CPSIA information can be obtained
at www.ICGtesting.com
Printed in the USA
LVHW021026250819
628859LV00034B/2024/P